Tangled Twins

Katherine Barnes

Copyright © 2015 Katherine Barnes
All rights reserved
First Edition

PAGE PUBLISHING, INC.
New York, NY

First originally published by Page Publishing, Inc. 2015

ISBN 978-1-68213-768-0 (pbk)
ISBN 978-1-68213-769-7 (digital)

Printed in the United States of America

Dedicated to my quirky twin sister, whose kidney disease tangled her up and death won

Most folks are like barbed wire fences...
They have their good points.

Unknown

CHAPTER 1

On November 15, 1960, a wintry wind blew brown crinkly leaves off oak branches in Bradberry, Vermont, and they fell into four inches of powdery snow.

Tabbie and Dorcas Thorndike, tenth graders at Bradberry High School, got ready to climb off their school bus at the end of East Hill Road.

Dorcas—the prima donna twin with red curly hair, freckles, and brown eyes—sat at the back of the bus. Growing up as a confident, strong-minded girl, she had set her mind on becoming an actress. When teachers, friends, and librarians asked her, "What do you want to be when you grow up?" she responded, "An actress, like my mother."

Last year, she detested the thirty-minute bus ride home; she tried to dissuade her dad and Aunt Phoebe from making her do it by using alternate, dramatic arguments. "Dad, I'm too old to ride with little squirts who tell knock-knock jokes and fall off their seats laughing." Or "Phoebe, it's unhealthy to sit with snotty-nosed kindergartners. I'll catch flu and spread it to you, Tabbie, and dad." Nothing worked, so her last plea was about her sister, Tabbie. "She's miserable. She becomes like an isolated, lonely owl who shuts her eyes to create darkness." Of course, Dorcas was lying, but it seemed that both her dad's and aunt's hearts were tied to Tabbie.

Nothing worked, and she and Tabbie were riding the bus again this year. She devised a creative alternative to solve her dilemma. Dorcas sat at the back of the ratty bus and placed a reserved sign across the entire row of seats.

For the first two weeks on the bus, she studied the students riding restlessly, elbowing seatmates and knocking knees against knees. On the third week, she tapped the shoulders of four girls and two boys and invited them to sit with her. She moved into the seat in front of them and turned backward facing them. As she looked at five eager faces and one shy one, she felt like the director of a play.

"Who likes to play pretend?"

Five right hands and one left one went up.

"Who knows what an actor is?"

Five pairs of bright eyes danced; beaming smiles turned into shouts, "I do. I do."

One face stayed serious, eyes looking down, no sound. I've chosen a Tabbie, she mused. Shall I send her to another seat? No, I'll let her stay. Maybe she has a wick that I can put a match to and she'll burst into flames.

"Go ahead," she said, and pointed to a freckled-faced, red-haired girl. A replica of myself, she thought, waiting for her to answer.

"An actor can be any person or animal she wants to be. If I want to be a mad mother, I scowl, scold, and shake my finger, 'You didn't make your bed.' I order, 'Go do it now, or you'll get a spanking.' I inspect to see if the bed is neat."

"Very good." Dorcas clapped. "What's your name?"

"Tammie."

Dorcas looked around at the other children. "Anyone else?"

She pointed to a dark-haired boy with large ears that poked out.

"My dad reads me fairy tales every night. I want to be Robin Hood and shoot bad guys." He pulled his arm back as if he were shooting a bow and arrow.

Dorcas smiled, seeing imagination, excitement, and energy popping up in front of her. "This week, I want you to ask your parents to read Peter Pan to you. Next week, I'll cast the parts."

Tabbie—the prettier, quieter twin, with brown hair and gray-green eyes—sat in the front of the bus with first and second graders whose boots barely touched the floor. She asked them about their day, their friends, schoolwork, and what they did during recess. One little girl, hiding in her coat, started crying.

"What's wrong?" Tabbie asked.

"Danny called me a dummy," the little girl sobbed.

Tabbie hugged her. "I'll tell you how to stop him. First, ignore him and walk away. If he keeps calling you that, say, 'I'm not listening to you.' If that doesn't work, go tell your teacher."

A frost flake on the bus window listening would be shocked to hear Tabbie give that answer.

The frost flake's question would be, "Why don't you stop your twin sister, Dorcas, from calling you a dummy?"

If Tabbie could hear the question, she might have said, "I try, but Dorcas insists on calling me stupid. She says I'll never be smart like her. She boasts about her A pluses and rubs my nose in my Cs and Ds. She thinks I should give up my dream of going to college and become a housewife or maid instead."

The frost flake might ask, "Why didn't anyone stop or punish her?"

"Dorcas does it when I am home, alone."

"Why don't you tell your dad or Aunt Phoebe about it?" the persistent frost flake might ask.

"They don't come home from their work at school until 5 p.m. and are worn out. Aunt Phoebe is principal of Bradberry Elementary School, and Dad teaches history at the high school."

The frost flake would weep and melt. How can one twin be so selfish and critical?

XXXXX

At five-thirty, Phoebe hurried into the mudroom, pulled off her boots (she was young-old and could balance herself without sitting on the bench), yanked off her blue scarf and hat (which she had knit), grabbed her schoolbag, and entered the living room. "Anyone home?" she yelled down the hall, hoping to see Tabbie's and Dorcas's doors open.

Dorcas looked out and waved. "Hi, Aunt Phoebe. I'm rereading *Peter Pan*. My kids on the bus are going to act that next week."

"Good." Phoebe waited for Tabbie's greeting, but Tabbie's door stayed closed.

She walked down and knocked. No answer. "Tabbie, can I come in?" she asked.

"I'd rather be alone," a soft, barely audible voice answered.

"How did your history test go, Tabbie?" Phoebe asked, opening the door slowly. For a week, her dad had reviewed battle dates, generals' names, and locations of World War II with her.

"I got a D," Tabbie whispered, looking up from her bed. The ceiling light was off. She felt defeated, like an American soldier losing a battle in Berlin. She had studied so hard for it, but her mind froze when she read the multiple-choice questions; she was better at essays.

She held her history book in her lap and was tearing pages out of it.

"Tabbie, stop!" Phoebe said, grabbing the book from her. "You're going to need those pages the rest of the year."

"Aunt Phoebe, why am I so dumb? Why did God make me this way? Why did Dorcas get all the brains?"

"Tabbie, you and Dorcas are different. Dorcas has a photographic memory, which means she looks at a page and remembers all the facts on it. Your mom is like that. You're more like your dad and me. We study and repeat what we read, and even then, we forget important facts when we are under pressure.

"When I was a freshman in college and having difficulty with multiple-choice tests, my roommate told me a trick. She said, 'Eliminate two choices right away, the foolish ones. Then make sentences with the other two. One will seem more accurate than the other one, so choose that one.' I wish I had known that in high school. I would have scored higher on my tests."

"I'll try that next time," Tabbie said. "Please don't tell Dorcas that I got a D on the test."

"I won't. Does reheated venison stew tantalize your taste buds?" Phoebe asked, opening the door.

Dorcas popped in. "I already know your grade, Tabbie. I was listening through the keyhole. I'm disappointed in you. Next time, I'll help you review instead of Dad. I won't take no for an answer."

Tabbie did what Dorcas wanted. Dorcas dictated their relationship. She was the timekeeper of how much time they spent together. When Tabbie didn't meet Dorcas's standards of being smart or lively and fun, Dorcas left Tabbie and phoned her actress friend Penelope. They read a play once a week, and Dorcas planned to call her tonight to discuss Tennessee Williams's *The Glass Menagerie*.

At six o'clock, Phoebe heard Richard stomping his boots in the mudroom, and she went out to meet him. She grabbed his sleeve and whispered, "Tabbie got a D on her history test. She is devastated and has drawn a stick figure of herself with derogatory names all over her paper—*stupid, moron, failure, dull, dummy*. Will you speak to her?"

He dropped his briefcase in his room at the end of the hall and came back to Tabbie's room. He knocked and called out, "Anybody home?"

Silence.

"Tabbie, it's Dad. I need a hug. Your morning one has run out." He waited. Then he heard a soft, barely audible voice.

"Dad, go away. You can spend your time in more valuable ways than with me."

"I disagree," he answered, turning the doorknob. When he entered, he saw Tabbie sitting on top of a mound of torn paper that she was trying to hide. "Will you stand up for a squeeze?" he asked. As she stood, he darted down to pick up the ripped sheets. "Tabbie, you've destroyed your history test and book!" His eyes grew wide. "We were going to look at those together."

"Dad, I failed it," she said, collapsing on the bed. "All the hours we spent reviewing the chapters didn't do any good. I'm a loser. Do you think you could hammer a hole in my brain and siphon some smart genes in there?"

"No, but I can tell you a story. When I was in ninth grade, I failed a math and history test. My teacher assigned a pretty tenth-grade tutor to help me. I met with her every week and began to pass my tests. Miracles do happen. Your dad is a high school history teacher now."

"Do you think I might be a history teacher someday?" Tabbie looked up into his kind face.

"Your life journey is just unfolding. You'll be good at whatever you choose." He hugged her and stood up. Someone was knocking on the door. "Oh, I forgot to tell you." He bent over and whispered, "My tutor, Sally, became my girlfriend."

They heard Dorcas's voice. "Dad, I'm home too. I want to show you my A+ that I got on my test."

Richard opened the door, turned toward Tabbie, and grinned. "Thanks, Dad. I feel better," she said, smiling back.

As Dorcas and her dad left her room, Tabbie heard him say, "That's great, honey. I don't see any mistakes."

Tabbie walked over to her wall mirror, looked in, scrunched her face into ugliness, and yanked a clump of her pretty brown hair. "I'll never hear him say that to me," she mumbled. Then she remembered the encouragements that he and Aunt Phoebe gave her. She stared into the mirror again, smoothed her face with her fingertips, brushed her hair, and smiled. "I'm good enough. Maybe I'll find an upper classmate to tutor me, and we'll start dating." She smiled, smelling the pepper and ketchup in Phoebe's venison stew, and headed toward the kitchen.

In January, as Tabbie moved from age fifteen to sixteen (her birthday was in March), her flat chest grew round, pubic hair sprouted black, and she grew to five feet seven inches. She had to replace her jerseys and jeans to size 12. Her breasts poking through her shirts embarrassed her.

Dorcas's breasts hadn't grown, so she teased Tabbie. "The boys are going to stare at you. You better not be in a room alone with them."

Her low grades discouraged her, and so did Dorcas's slingshot words. One time, when Tabbie brought a history test to the dining room table to show everyone her B-, Dorcas got up, found a pencil in the kitchen drawer, and wrote on it, "Good effort, but let your sister help you study next time. She's an A student." Dorcas looked at her dad. "I think you need to take Tabbie to a doctor who studies brains so he can tell us what's wrong."

"I'll think about it, Dorcas. I may take you along and ask him to examine you to find out why you are so stubborn."

"That would be a waste of money. Redheads are always stubborn, and I get it from my mother."

Richard tutored and talked to Tabbie often.

"Dad, do you think anyone will hire me to work this summer?" she asked frequently. She loved his response.

"You'll have more offers than bees have blossoms."

It became a duet for them, and they played it often.

The other melody around Tabbie's neck became a smart, handsome eleventh-grade student named Thomas. One day in the noisy cafeteria, she was eating her slaw dog and pushing aside the chili beans. He came over, slipped into the chair beside her, and said, "You and I must be kin. I detest beans also. If I eat a helping, suddenly people desert me as if I were a leper." He smiled. "Sorry, that's a strange introduction, but I'm Thomas Houston. I've admired you from a distance since the first day of school."

Tabbie smiled. "Are you sure you didn't eat some beans at a different table? You smell a little funny." She felt warm inside; she was proud of making a joke.

After their first meeting, he sought her everywhere; he appeared outside her classroom door and walked her to her next class; they ate lunch together, and sometimes he surprised her by waiting outside of the girls' bathroom. He had begun to hold and squeeze her hand.

One day he told her, "You're pretty. Will you go with me?"

"Yes." Tabbie smiled, feeling all the labels that Dorcas had given her—dumb, boring, a people pleaser—loosen and fly into the wind. She felt clean and ready to replace them with Thomas's words: "Pretty, kind, special, and loveable."

Dorcas became jealous that Tabbie had a boyfriend. She didn't want one, but she didn't want Tabbie to have one. She increased her criticisms and pejorative labels. "Tabbie, you're embarrassing me at school. When they post grades on the hall bulletin board, yours are always C or C minus."

Tabbie often sought comfort from Phoebe. "Oh, Aunt Phoebe, I'm tired of Dorcas calling me stupid. If I pray enough, do you think God will change my brain cells for smarter ones and give her mine?"

Phoebe smiled, shook her head, and hugged Tabbie. "God doesn't harm people or take away their talents. He blesses us as we are. He has plans for you and will reveal them as you grow."

Tabbie also confided in Thomas now that they were dating. When they were alone outdoors, as she was waiting for her bus, she whispered, "As I was falling asleep last night, Dorcas opened my door and whispered, 'You're still going to fail your tests. Your new boyfriend can't take them for you.'"

"Did you stand up to her?" he asked.

She shook her head. "Tonight I'm going to lock my bedroom door," she said, smiling, pleased with her idea.

Thomas grew fierce. "Call her a mythomane. You know how my mother, who is a dictionary maniac, gives me a new word to memorize each day. She gave me that one last week. It means 'egomaniac, self-promoting, and a person who exaggerates and lies.' That describes Dorcas."

"I'll try, Thomas," Tabbie said as the bus pulled up to the curb. She turned and whispered, "I love you."

Dorcas pushed in front of her and climbed up the steps.

"Tigress, beware. I've called the Wild Game Department to come and capture you," Thomas said, walking off.

XXXXX

By March, Tabbie's grades were climbing to Bs while Dorcas's reached A++.

The week before spring break, which was the beginning of April, teachers gave end of the unit tests in English and math. On Friday, Dorcas and Tabbie received their grades. At supper that night, Tabbie circulated her papers; she had gotten a B+ in English and a B in math. Phoebe and Richard clapped, hooted, and hollered. Dorcas remained quiet. Then she passed her tests around: A++. "Excellent" capped each sheet.

As they finished their meal, Dorcas said, "I'm going next door to Aunt Bess's. She told me she would pay me $10 for each A+ on my test."

Richard looked over at Dorcas. "Dorcas, it's getting late. It's already eight thirty. You have an hour at Bess's. Watch out for coyotes. They hunt her cats at this time of night."

"Here, take this flashlight," Tabbie said, handing her a red plastic one.

"Be home at nine thirty, Dorcas," Phoebe said.

"I will, and if I'm late, you can call me."

"Dorcas, you are old enough to take responsibility to return on time. If you're late, you will be grounded," Richard said.

As Dorcas put on her red jacket, cap, and matching gloves, she opened the door and dashed across the thin layer of ice to her Aunt Bess's log cabin. Aunt Bess, Phoebe's sister, had left her pharmacy job in Connecticut when the twins were in second grade. "You need my help," she had said, building her cabin next to Phoebe's and Richard's home. Dorcas became her favorite niece.

As Phoebe rinsed the dishes, Tabbie dried them, and Richard put them away. Then he asked, "Who wants to bet that Dorcas comes home on time?"

"I think she'll be late," Phoebe said, and she'll make up one hundred excuses.

"Does anyone want to guess what they will be?" Phoebe said.

"Bess's clocks weren't working," Richard said.

"Her cat, Miniwheat, was on the counter eating the brownies that she had made for Dorcas, so she had to defrost the extras that she had frozen," Phoebe said.

Tabbie said, "She'll argue that her A++s earned her half an hour extra. Will you excuse me, please? I'm going to my room to start reading *Wuthering Heights*. We're reading that after spring break."

Richard settled in his brown recliner chair. "Phoebe, will you turn the TV on to the Boston Channel? We may get a history special."

Ten minutes later, he was snoring.

Phoebe watched the story of *Sherman's March to the Sea* on TV.

At nine thirty, Tabbie came out of her room, sucking on a cherry lollipop.

"Do you want one?" She offered several to Phoebe and her dad.

They turned them down, and six eyes looked up at the mantle clock.

The hands pointed to 9:30 p.m. Their eyes turned to the door. No one was there. The phone didn't ring.

"What do we do now?" Tabbie asked, looking at Phoebe and her dad.

"If you were a parent, Tabbie, what would you do?" Phoebe asked.

Tabbie hesitated. "I'd make her do something she hated, like vacuuming and dusting the whole house tomorrow."

"We could add washing sheets and towels," Phoebe said.

"How about mopping the kitchen and bathroom floors and scrubbing the toilets?" Richard said.

They heard the doorknob turn and looked at the clock. It was 9:50 p.m. The door opened, and a sobbing Dorcas fell on the floor. The knees of her jeans were torn. Blood seeped through the tears. "Ouch, I need a doctor," she wailed.

"You're twenty minutes late, Dorcas," Richard said sternly.

Dorcas looked up at Phoebe. "Help me, Aunt Phoebe. I was running across the lawn so I wouldn't be late. I slipped on ice. Look how I hurt myself." She slid her pants down and showed everyone her sores.

Phoebe looked at them closely and went to the bathroom to get a clean cloth and alcohol. When she returned, she knelt down and carefully rubbed the cuts.

"Ouch!" Dorcas screamed. "I'm sorry, Aunt Phoebe. It stings. Going through this misery, I'm wiser," she said dramatically. "From now on, I'll leave Bess's on time." Dorcas stayed on the floor, covering her legs with her jacket. "Tabbie, will you get my pajama bottoms please, the red ones?"

When Tabbie returned, Dorcas asked, "Will you help me put them on?"

"No, Dorcas, you can do that."

Dorcas stared at Tabbie with surprise. "What's wrong with you? You've always done what I've told you to do."

Tabbie stood up tall. "I'm starting to learn that I can say no to you. No, no, no." She felt free each time she said it. She felt like a canary freed from her cage, flying high, making it impossible for a cat or her sister to capture her.

Tabbie made a pact to herself never to be caught in her sister's tangle again.

CHAPTER 2

On Saturday morning of spring break, Tabbie planned to sleep late, at least past 7:00 a.m. (her school day habit). Different parts of Tabbie's body, legs, and arms lay in sluggish positions on her bed. Her blue wool blanket covered her completely, from her tangled hair to her curled toes.

At 7:00 a.m., she heard her door open, footsteps tiptoeing toward her bed, and suddenly, an alarm rang loudly in her ears. Her eyes opened, and she saw Dorcas above her; her right arm awoke, and she knocked the clock out of Dorcas's hand. "Get out, I'm sleeping late this morning."

"Tabbie," Dorcas said, pulling Tabbie's covers off and tossing jeans, a green sweatshirt, and sneakers on top of her. "Rise and shine, and be quick about it. We have to clean the house this morning. I'm going to go to Penelope's for lunch."

Tabbie sat, rubbing her eyes and shaking her head. "You've got it wrong, sister. You're cleaning, and I'm going to Thomas's house. He's going to tutor me in math."

Dorcas turned to Tabbie's desk, took her sister's math book, and stuck it under her shirt. "No math, no Thomas."

Tabbie jumped up on her bed and reached for Dorcas's shirt. Dorcas backed up, Tabbie plunged toward her, the heavy book slipped out and Tabbie fell on the floor. She banged her nose on the math book, which was thick as a brick, and it started bleeding. She squeezed her nose, hoping to stop the outpour. She felt a large bump. "Please get me a towel, Dorcas, and call Dad or Phoebe. I think I've broken my nose."

"Lie down, Tabbie, your blood is spurting everywhere, and I have to clean in here today!" Dorcas left the room, and a minute later, Phoebe and her dad appeared.

"What happened, Tabbie?" Phoebe ran over and knelt beside her.

"Are you responsible for this, Dorcas?" Richard looked at her.

"Why do you always blame me, Dad?" Dorcas said, stomping off.

"Tabbie, we're going to have to take you to the emergency room to get your nose examined," Phoebe said, pulling out a clean red shirt from her bureau. "Richard, please help her stand and walk to the car. I'll drive her. You stay here and keep Dorcas to her task of cleaning."

Dorcas, who had returned said, "I think you're overreacting, Aunt Phoebe. If it were me, you'd wait an hour or half a day to see the seriousness of the injury. You baby Tabbie. It's not good for her, that's why she's a sissy. She needs to grow strong and tough."

"Dorcas, I would do the same for you, but you probably wouldn't let me. You know how you dislike doctors. In fact, you've been known to hide from them! Remember the time Dr. Otley made a home visit to check your fire-red throat? You hid under your bed, and no one could find you."

Tabbie's nose started bleeding again as Richard walked her to the car.

Dorcas handed Tabbie a dark-blue towel. "We need to buy red ones, Aunt Phoebe, if Tabbie continues to bleed like a creek. I think we should throw this one away rather than wash it."

"Sounds like a good idea, Dorcas," Richard said, helping Tabbie into the car. Phoebe and Dorcas followed.

"Wait, Richard. Dorcas, will you bring me some garbage bags, please," Phoebe said.

To Phoebe's amazement, Dorcas went inside and came back with four of them.

"Thank you, Dorcas, that's kind of you."

"Please don't say *kind*. That's Tabbie's word. Say *thoughtful*."

"Hand them to your dad, Dorcas, and he will put them across the seat so that blood doesn't drip on my upholstery."

"I can do it, Aunt Phoebe. I am trying to be more thoughtful. Then I can add that to my college résumé. I know you don't like to lie, so if you see me acting helpful, then you can add that as one of my good qualities on the parent form and be truthful. Mother can add that I'm a gifted actress." Dorcas looked at Tabbie. "What would you say about me, sister?"

"Dorcas, stop talking and put the bags on the seat. We have to go," Phoebe said, pushing her slightly so she could help Tabbie in.

Dorcas lay two bags across Tabbie's lap. "Done," she said. "I get an A+ for my behavior. Would you agree, Dad?"

He nodded. "I hope we continue to reap that behavior. Your aunt Phoebe and I sowed the seeds many years ago. They've taken a long time to sprout." He kissed Tabbie, saying, "I hope it's not broken. I love you." Then he put his arm on Dorcas' shoulder. "It's time to go in and clean the house."

Phoebe drove carefully around the curves on East Hill Road. When she reached the bottom of the road, she stopped, looked both ways, and drove across Route 30 into the Otley Hospital emergency room, which was at the back of the building.

It was a small ten-bed hospital ruled over by Dr. George Otley. He had a reputation as being "Hitler of the hospital." He raised funds to build it, cut the red ribbon at the opening in 1950, and practiced there as the only doctor.

In the spring every year, when medical students graduated from the University of Vermont and New Hampshire, he dressed in a striped suit, a red bow tie, and a brown corduroy cap and drove his red convertible to the graduations to recruit doctors. When he described Bradberry's small population and treating farmers' fractures from falling off tractors and high school students' broken bones from football injuries, most doctors declined.

"What about more complicated problems like strokes or kidney disease?" they would ask.

"We send them to Glennsboro, thirty miles south of here, a larger hospital with more modern equipment." As a result of Dr. Otley's honest description, the graduates chose to go elsewhere.

On Saturday, when Phoebe arrived with Tabbie, Dr. Otley, dressed in his recruiting outfit, greeted them at the door.

"Ms. Thorndike." He went toward Phoebe and shook her hand. "My wife, Sharon, finds it delightful teaching fifth-grade students in your school. She has invited me to come bring a skeleton and show the children the bones under our body parts. I won't get into the difference between ladies and men." He smiled and winked.

"Has Tabbie hurt herself?" he asked, bending down to examine Tabbie's swollen, crooked nose, which was turning purple. He had treated both twins since age five when their mother left them and Richard and Phoebe began rearing them. "Looks like you've broken your nose, young girl. Did your sister hit you?"

Tabbie shook her head. Blood dripped out of her nostrils.

"The town gossip is that your twin sister is a copy of your mother, Kate: difficult to deal with a haughty young woman. Is that right, Tabbie?"

She shrugged. She had never liked Dr. Otley. He talked more than treated.

"Has your mother ever called or visited you since she and her actor friend returned to the United States from England?"

Tabbie ignored him and asked, "Are you going to set my nose?"

"Of course," he said. He called his nurse, Sarah, who took Tabbie to a hospital bed behind a curtain. "You can come in here with us, Phoebe," he said, opening the curtain.

He motioned to Tabbie to lie down. "Give me a roll of gauze, Sarah."

She handed him a white roll, which he unwound and packed into Tabbie's nose. "Do you want to be a nurse, Tabbie?" he asked as he worked.

She couldn't talk; she could hardly breathe. She shrugged her shoulders.

"Phoebe, my secretary will call you Monday to tell you the cost of this simple fix. Tabbie, come back in two weeks, and I'll unpack you. Until then, don't let your sister bang you up." He left the room.

On the way home, Tabbie pulled the rear-view mirror close to her. She looked in it and gasped. "I look like a thug. Thomas will ditch me when he sees me looking like this."

"Of course he won't. He likes all of you, inside and out," Phoebe said.

Tabbie blushed; she hoped that Phoebe didn't know that she and Thomas were smooching.

"Do I have to go to school on Monday?" Tabbie asked. "Kids are going to tease me."

"Tabbie, you've forgotten, next week is spring break. The following week, when you return to school, your nose will be less swollen. You'll look like a softball player who ran after a whizzing ball to catch it and the ball hit your nose."

"You've got quite an imagination, Aunt Phoebe," Tabbie said.

"Didn't I tell you that your grandmother, Carole, who was my sister, and I used to take turns making up stories," Phoebe said, pulling into the drive way.

As they entered the house, Dorcas greeted them with a dustrag. She screamed. "Tabbie, you look like a goat who has crashed into a tractor!"

"Dorcas, you look like a farmer's wife with a sixth-grade education!" Tabbie said. "Did you clean my room?" She went down the hallway to see. Her head ached, and she wanted to lie down and sleep.

XXXXX

The day before Easter, Tabbie went to see Dr. Otley, and he pulled the gauze out of her nose.

"Who are you having for Easter?" he asked. Phoebe had found over the years that she had to be cautious answering his questions. One year he had invited himself for Easter. His wife had gone out of town to look after her sick mother, and he didn't want to eat alone.

"We are having a crowd. The girls and Richard are having guests, and my sister, Bess, is coming."

"Do you mind my asking whether Kate and her husband are coming? The gossip around town is that you invited them and she declined."

"That's correct," Phoebe said, as she and Tabbie left his office.

Once in the car, Tabbie sat forward and looked in the rear-view mirror. "My nose looks less puffy, but the bruise is still there." She sighed. She turned to Phoebe and asked, "Who starts the gossip in town?"

"Someone who doesn't have anything to do."

"I hope Dr. Otley doesn't come uninvited. He would spoil our fun."

XXXXX

On Easter Night, Tabbie put on her new pale green linen dress with crocheted yellow daisies on the collar and belt. She looked at herself in the mirror and smiled. "I wish I had daisy perfume," she said, half joking.

Richard's friend Cindy, a young teacher with long blond hair, came early, carrying a lemon meringue pie and a hot apple pie smelling of cinnamon and brown sugar. Richard took them both into the kitchen.

Phoebe looked at Cindy and smiled. She had curled her hair into a pageboy and wore an orange sweater and orange skirt.

"Welcome, I hardly recognize you," Phoebe said. "You're usually in black pants and dark shirts at school."

"Second graders have chalk, food, or snot on their hands, so I try to dress in clothes that are easy to wash," Cindy said. "Richard, it's good to see you." She went over to kiss his cheek. He had already pinched pieces off both pies, and a chunk of apple and a smear of whipped meringue stuck to his lips. She picked them off and asked, "Was it good?"

"Delicious."

The back door opened, and Bess came bumbling in, carrying a hot green bean casserole and a cut glass saucer with celery and carrots in it. She tripped on the small throw rug by the door. Richard caught her before she fell. Tabbie reached for the casserole, and Cindy took her arm and seated her on a kitchen chair.

Thomas and Penelope arrived at the same time. Phoebe and her kitchen crew left the kitchen to greet them. Penelope was carrying a straw basket filled with biscuits. She handed them to Phoebe. "Thank you for inviting me, Ms. Phoebe. Where's Dorcas?"

"She's dressing in her room. Please go down and tell her it's time to come."

Thomas stepped up to Phoebe and handed her a pan of corn bread muffins. "My mother made these for you."

"Thank you, Thomas. Why don't you and Tabbie go into the kitchen and scoop them out of the tin? Put them on our Wedgwood plate, Tabbie."

They went into the kitchen, with only an inch between them. They stood at the sink together, loosening the muffins onto the plate and scouring the tin with Brillo. They bumped bottoms and splashed soapy water on each other's faces.

"Ouch," Tabbie said, closing her right eye, where soap had slipped under her lashes. "It stings. Thomas, please get it out of my eye."

"Bend," he said, laying her head back in the sink. "Open your eyes," he directed and poured a full glass of water on her face. "If we could shower together, I could help more," he whispered.

"Thomas, pull me up please," she said, trying to stand. He wrapped his arms around her and lifted. As Tabbie steadied her feet on the wet floor, she heard voices in the dining room exclaim, "Dorcas, how pretty you look."

Tabbie opened the door a crack and saw her red-haired sister in a tight red dress covered with sparkly beads.

Thomas peeked at her also. "Where did she get that? Has she visited a whorehouse?"

"She received a package from Kate last week. She probably bought it for Dorcas."

Tabbie squeezed Thomas's hand. "I used to be the pretty twin, and she was the smart one. Now she's beautiful and brainy...and I'm left with nothing."

"Stop, Tabbie." He leaned over to kiss her. "You're beautiful and smart. Since I've started tutoring you in math and history, you've made higher grades on your tests."

"Thanks for reminding me, Romeo," she said, taking his hand. They walked into the dining room together.

Phoebe smiled. "Now we're all here, let's sit down and eat. Please find your place cards."

They searched the small cardboard rabbit cards for their names. The table looked lovely; a white linen cloth covered the table, and the flames of the lavender candles in the candelabra danced and lit up the polished silver.

Cindy placed the turkey in front of Richard, who picked up his sharp knife and fork and started carving. He passed the plates down to Phoebe at the other end, and she spooned hot, buttery mashed potatoes and Tabbie's apple-cranberry dish, loaded with oatmeal and brown sugar topping on them. Bess, sitting next to Phoebe, slid her green bean casserole on the full dishes, and soon, everyone had a plate of delicious-smelling food in front of them.

Tabbie, who was sitting beside Bess, offered her corn bread.

Bess shook her head. "Corn bread goes with venison stew, not turkey," she said loudly, reaching for a roll. A large person like Bess couldn't speak softly.

Tabbie rubbed Thomas's leg under the table in case he felt badly because he had brought them. "I like corn bread any time," she emphasized.

Dorcas, seated across the table, said, "I'd steal for it."

Penelope added, "Yummy."

Cindy said, "I crave corn bread once a week."

Bess looked around the table. "I guess I'm the odd woman out."

As everyone picked up their knives and forks, Phoebe interrupted, "Richard, will you say grace, please?"

"We thank you, God, for our family gathering. May we share love and kindness with each other."

The next sounds were of knives clicking on china plates, forks filling mouths, and voices saying, "Wonderful."

As Phoebe offered everyone another spoonful of apple cranberry, she heard someone knocking on the door. "Who could that be?" she asked. "Dorcas, will you answer it, please?"

Dorcas went over and opened it. Kate and her husband, Ronald, were standing on the porch.

Dorcas stepped out and pulled the door closed. "What are you doing here?" The alarm in her voice sounded like a siren set off.

"Our plan to go to England fizzled out. Rather than spend Easter alone, we came here."

"I don't think you are still invited," Dorcas whispered.

"Of course, we are. We're family." Kate pushed past Dorcas and went inside. Ronald followed. Kate had dressed him in a navy blue coat, a red tie, and black pants. She was wearing red velvet pants, a white satin blouse, and a red vest.

Dorcas brought them into the dining area. "We have two uninvited guests. Shall we welcome them?"

Silence. Shock. Eating stopped.

"For those of you who don't know me, I'm Kate Thorndike Ryan." She pulled Ronald in. "I have an ex-husband there"—she pointed at Richard—"and a new one here." She pushed Ronald forward. "He's a well-known actor and producer of plays at Hepburn College."

Richard looked across the space. "Welcome, Ronald." He turned to Kate. "If I let you in, you'll have to promise to be pleasant and polite. The first rude word, and you're out."

Dorcas whispered in Penelope's ear, "And the drama begins."

Kate curtsied and repeated herself, "Let me introduce myself for those who don't know me. I'm the queen bee from Richard's old hive." She walked behind him, and her fingers buzzed above him. "And who are you?" she asked, staring at Cindy.

"I am Cindy Matthews, his girlfriend."

Kate stooped beside Cindy and whispered loudly, "Do you want me to share the good and the bad about the man you are dating?"

Cindy said, "No thank you. I like to form my own opinions."

Phoebe looked over at Kate. "We don't have room for you and Ronald at the table. It's full. We can put you in the kitchen."

"Don't the younger ones give up their seats to the older generation?" Kate tapped Thomas on his shoulder. "You're a stranger. Please move."

Tabbie whipped around and addressed Kate. "He's a friend of mine and has more privileges here than you do, Kate." Tabbie stood up and looked directly into Kate's brown eyes. "Kate, when are you going to grow up and consider others? You are a guest in this house. Guests don't order people around."

Kate looked over at her. "Is that you, Tabbie? You used to be as timid as a snail, always withdrawing inside. You seem different now. Is this young man you are dating"—she jabbed her finger at Thomas—"giving you the confidence and courage that Dorcas carved away?"

Dorcas looked across the table at Kate. "Kate, watch what you say! You are to blame for both Tabbie's and my shortcomings. You abandoned us at age five. How could you? I was a cute curly redheaded little girl who was running and exploring everywhere and talking nonstop. Tabbie was sweet and kind, sucked on her thumb, twirled her hair, and gave me whatever I wanted."

Kate grew furious listening to Dorcas. "I don't have to hear this. Dorcas, go to your room."

"No. I don't have to listen to you. This is my house, not yours."

Phoebe looked down the table at Richard. "Stop this," she mouthed.

Richard stood and said, "Phoebe worked hard to make this Easter meal special. Kate, you are ruining it. You can leave now." He looked at Dorcas, who had started to say something. "Don't say a word," he said.

"We are leaving now," Kate said, leading Ronald to the door. Richard followed to prevent her from coming back. "Your request has no power over me. I'd stay if I wanted, but we had another invitation from a fellow faculty member at Hepburn."

She looked down at Phoebe. "I'm sorry, Phoebe. There's a full moon tonight, which makes me wild."

"And crazy," Richard added.

"I'll visit you and the twins when it's a quarter moon." She waved and walked through the door.

Phoebe smiled and said, "Peace again."

Bess scowled, saying, "She is a rude, ditzy woman. Phoebe, why didn't you pick up her up by those red velvet pants and throw her out?"

"I didn't need to. Richard did it. Let's eat our dessert and omit any conversation about her."

"Everyone, stay seated, and Thomas and I will clear the table," Tabbie said.

"Penelope and I will bring the pies out," Dorcas said.

"Do you have vanilla ice cream to scoop on top?" Bess asked. "I think the sweetness of dessert will dissolve any memories of Kate's disastrous visit."

CHAPTER 3

Spring in Bradberry bloomed apple blossoms, sweet-smelling lilacs, and tiny green maple leaves with plans to grow. Warmer days delighted everyone.

The last two months of school, Thomas and Tabbie were like interlacing orchid roots. On weekends, they hiked and ate picnics in fields bordered by pungent pines, light-green leaves of hemlocks, and bolder greens of maples. Small clearings in evergreen woods beside streams rippling over rocks gave privacy for kissing, touching, and tickling.

In June, Tabbie and Dorcas passed their exams and became seniors; Thomas received his diploma. Tabbie felt sad that they wouldn't be sharing lunch at school or truck rides home next year, but she was proud that he graduated with honors. She sat beside his parents, who were whooping and hollering; she clapped loudly and long until the palms of her hands stung and became red. After the graduation speech, which was delivered by Principal Lander's older brother who taught philosophy at Dartmouth, the graduates spread out to find their families. Thomas had seen his parents and Tabbie in the third row, and he rushed over to hug them.

"Good job, son," his father said, clapping him on his back. "Enjoy summer because the studying starts all over again in September. In college the professors will expect more of you."

His mother, Margaret, focused on the moment. "You looked so handsome and grown-up on stage. I'm sorry that your brother missed it, but he is digging up ancient artifacts at Macchu Pichu in Peru. I'll take pictures to send to him. Tabbie, you stand beside Thomas. I don't think Dan knows what you look like."

"Hurry, Margaret. We have to beat all the other families to Bob's Burgers. Otherwise we'll spend half an hour in line. We'll ride in my car," Thomas's dad said. He led them to a parking space in front of the school that said "Reserved for Dr. Houston."

"How did you rate this, Dad?" Thomas asked.

"Next week I'm giving your principal, Mr. Landers, a whitening treatment for his teeth, filling four cavities, and putting braces on him. He needed them when he was younger, but his parents refused to spend their money. I'm doing all this work for a pittance."

"Mr. Landers is going to look comical in braces when he stands in front of the school for morning announcements," Thomas said, as his father sped to Bob's, twenty minutes away. Bob made huge burgers and customers' jaws sometimes came unhinged as they opened their mouths to bite into the burger. After finishing fries and homemade chips, Thomas's dad took them back to the school, where Thomas's truck was parked.

"Thanks, Dad. Tabbie and I will spend the rest of the day together. I'll be home at eleven o'clock." As they drove off, Thomas said to Tabbie, "How about driving to the creek?"

"It's too wet, Thomas. It has been raining for a week. The tires will sink into the mud and we'll be stuck. Remember, tomorrow I start my new job, helping Cindy with her six-week summer program at the elementary school. She asked me to make name tags for the students. I don't want to get stuck in the mud or in your arms. Let's hang out at my house this afternoon."

At seven o'clock that night, Tabbie shooed Thomas away. "I have to call Cindy and ask her what else I can do for her."

"I'll let you go if you promise to give me your body tomorrow night," he said. He handed her a pad of paper and pen. "I want it in writing."

"I'm going to share myself, not give it away. Remember, you're teaching me to be independent and claim myself."

"That's with Dorcas, not with me. I'm the exception," he said, kissing her.

When Thomas left, Tabbie called Cindy at home. "Cindy, can I do any last minute things for you? I want to make sure I have the children's names right. Are Doodle Bug and Monster correct?"

"Yes. If you could make twenty-five sheets of paper, with name, address, and telephone numbers on them, I'd appreciate it."

"No problem, Cindy. I'll be at school at seven thirty tomorrow morning to help you set up."

"Thanks, Tabbie. We have fifteen boys and ten girls. I'm going to need your help with the boys. Five are troublemakers, and their mothers are sending them to my class to keep them away from home."

Over the next week, Tabbie found firm ways to get their cooperation. She liked bending down to their level, singing in a Cindy voice "You've done good, you've understood," and putting a happy-face sticker on their papers.

The first and second graders left at noon; in the afternoons, Tabbie helped Cindy make math sheets for the next day. As they squeezed into the students' small desks, their knees bumped, and papers fell on the floor. Cindy leaned over the desk to pick them up and toppled over it, like a monkey. After laughing, Tabbie helped her stand, and they moved to Cindy's taller desk in front of the room.

"Do you dream, Cindy?" Tabbie asked, as she switched a red crayon for a blue one.

"Some nights, last night I dreamed that two frogs were sitting on a lily pad, sticking out their tongues at each other, and floating down a river. They were cute."

"I don't mean that kind of dream," Tabbie said. "I mean visions of the future.

Do you see yourself in a different place, happy, and doing something you've always hoped for?"

Cindy nodded. "I visualize living in your home someday with Richard, Phoebe, and you and Dorcas." She smiled at Tabbie.

"I dream about becoming a teacher and marrying Thomas," Tabbie whispered.

Cindy beamed. "I can see both of those happening," she said, hugging Tabbie.

XXXXX

Thomas spent the summer working at the Retreat Dairy Farm, shoveling manure out of barns, feeding hay to Holsteins, and riding a tractor cutting grass. He came home hot and exhausted. After drinking several root beers, washing up, and dabbing his neck with his dad's cologne, he joined Tabbie and her aunt Phoebe for burgers and corn on the cob most evenings. Sweet watermelon and oatmeal cookies were the grand finales.

After they helped Phoebe clean up the kitchen, they walked through the fields, picking daisies, pulling the petals off, and playing the game "He Loves Me, He Loves Me Not." Tabbie kept at it until her bare flower ended at "He loves me." She squeezed Thomas's hand as they approached their clearing in the pinewoods. They stepped over a low stonewall, brushed some pine cones off their soft pine needle bed, and lowered their blue blanket and themselves. They lay sideways, fitting breasts to chest and winding legs around each other. Tabbie moved slightly and touched Thomas's face and neck. Thomas unbuttoned her shirt, unfastened her bra, and kneaded her breasts.

"Can we do it tonight?" she asked, touching his zipper.

"Remember, we said we were going to wait." Thomas held her as the sky darkened. "We better get back before it's so black that we can't see." He helped her up and kissed her. "Remember the time you fell over a root and hurt your ankle? I don't want that to happen again."

XXXXX

The summer weeks passed quickly. Tabbie, who was keeping track of time, reminded Thomas the last segment of August. "We have two more weeks together before you go to college and I start my senior year. Now our jobs are over, we can spend twenty-four hours a day together, at least our waking hours. At night, we will sleep in our own rooms. Maybe the last night we could go to a motel in Glennsboro and share the same bed," she suggested.

"If you still want to spend time with me," he said softly, helping her climb over the stonewall.

"Of course I do. When you're off at college, I'll write you every day, and we can talk on the phone on weekends." Tears spilled down her cheeks and throat. "I'm going to miss you," she said, kissing him again.

The next evening, Thomas picked up Tabbie at seven o'clock, and they went to Pete's Pizza in a neighboring town. She looked beautiful, her light-brown hair falling below her neck and her green eyes matching her sweater. Thomas drove quietly. Tabbie squeezed his hand.

"Things are changing in my life, Tabbie." He wriggled his wrist to loosen her grip.

"What's wrong?" she asked, feeling scared and biting her lip.

"Let's wait until we get inside Pete's." He pulled into the parking lot, found a spot, and turned off the motor. Usually, he leaned over, kissed her and whispered, "Stay right here until I open the door for my princess." Tonight, he didn't do this.

She climbed out of the truck by herself and joined him as he started walking toward the restaurant door. She took his hand and looked up at him. "You're acting differently tonight, Thomas." Her thoughts whirred until she came up with her worst fear. "Do you have another girlfriend?" she asked.

He shook his head.

They walked across the parking lot, the gravel crushing loudly under their feet. Once inside, he asked for a table in the center of the room. "The noisier the better," he whispered to the waitress, who was wiping a table with a dishrag.

Tabbie tipped her head back, looking up at him in a perplexed way. "What about our quiet table in the corner?"

"Can't you see it's taken?" he answered crossly, following the waitress to a table in the middle of the room.

"We could wait until those people leave. They're eating their dessert now."

"No, Tabbie. I've chosen this table, and we are going to sit here."

"I don't like your choice," Tabbie said, surprised and pleased that she stood up to him.

"I'm paying tonight, and I choose this one," he argued.

He didn't come over to pull her chair out, so she did it herself. She looked across the table and asked, "What's wrong?"

Thomas looked down at his silverware, crossed and uncrossed his feet underneath the table. He knocked his knees together for extra strength. He didn't want to break her heart, but he had to. "Tabbie, University of Vermont is a long way off, and I'm going to have to study weekends to keep my grades up to compete for medical school." He hesitated and studied her face. "We're going to have to stop dating."

"You're what?" she asked in disbelief, which turned to anger. "You can't stop dating me now. We're in love."

"I've got to think of my future, Tabbie. I'm not that smart, and my dreams are big. I'll probably need tutoring and lots of extra studying time."

"I've got big dreams also, of going to college, becoming a teacher, and marrying you. Remember in July we went to Glennsboro to look at an engagement ring? You put down a small deposit on the diamond heart-shaped one. Have you been pulling me along, as if I were a willing, docile dog? I no longer trust you. You're a liar!" She looked at him, with tears and a scowl staining her face.

"Tabbie, I didn't expect this type of reaction from you!" he said in disbelief and anger.

She hesitated, wondering if she was being too rude and defiant. Her heart felt sad. *Should I show it? No, I'm going to be stoic,* she decided. She could feel herself change her vision, looking at herself from a distance. *He's losing me; I'm not losing him! He's going to discover his mistake when he gets on campus.* She straightened her posture and said, "Thomas, you're going to regret your decision. Think it over while I go to the bathroom."

When she returned, she looked into his brown eyes; they seemed dark and resolute. She looked at the menu and then closed it. "You can take me home, Thomas."

In the truck she said to him, "You're not going to find anyone like me at the University of Vermont. I'm pretty, smart, and determined to do well at Vermont State Teacher's College." She was finally using and partly believing the affirmations he had taught her.

When she went into the house, she smelled grilled chicken and garlic and heard clanging of pots. She looked into the kitchen, and Phoebe was at the sink washing dishes. "Something smells good," she said, walking up to hug her.

"I cooked something to eat. Your dad and Cindy are out. There's a chicken breast and green beans left over, but you must be full of pizza."

"I'm fine," Tabbie said, not wanting to tell her about leaving the pizza house without eating. *I'll sneak in later to snack*, she told herself. *No, I won't. I'm not Dorcas, that's what she would do.*

"I'm going to bed, Aunt Phoebe. Sleep well," Tabbie said, going down the hall.

In her bedroom, she picked up her silver mirror on her bureau, looked into it, and talked to herself. "Smile, Tabbie. You told Thomas to buzz off and leave you alone." She tried smiling and couldn't. "Have I made a mistake?" she asked herself, feeling faint. "No, the ending would be the same. He started it, and I ended it." She breathed in deeply and smiled. "You're a new Tabbie, strong and confident."

After washing her face and putting on her favorite apple pajamas, she climbed into bed with *The Great Gatsby*, which was required reading for senior English.

The kitchen phone rang. Phoebe knocked on the door. "It's for you," she said.

"Who is it?" she asked.

"Thomas."

Should I talk to him? Tabbie wondered. Her old self would have run to the phone. *What should I do?* Her new self wondered. "It won't hurt to talk to him," she told herself.

She walked into the kitchen and took the phone from Phoebe. "You can go," she whispered, not wanting Phoebe to know about their breakup. When Phoebe left, she said, "Thomas, I thought we were done talking. What do you want?"

"To tell you that the first month I'm gone, I'll send you weekly postcards reminding you that you're the lovely, brave princess and Dorcas is the wicked one."

"Don't send me a card, Thomas. If you do, I'll tear it up without reading it."

"I'll never forget you, Tabbie," he said, hanging up.

"I'll never forget you, Thomas, but you'll never know it," she said into the dead line.

CHAPTER 4

Tabbie's feelings tumbled like somersaults the first day of school. *It's going to be strange without Thomas, strange and sad, but I can be strong without him.*

She woke up at six thirty on Monday morning, shivering because Phoebe didn't turn the gas furnace on until the end of September. She crawled deeper under her four blankets. She had been awake all night imagining slapping Thomas and banging a frying pan on his head because he left for University of Vermont last week without calling her to say good-bye. She wanted to add another blanket and sleep all day, maybe waking up at lunch for chicken noodle soup and crackers. *Nothing good will happen today*, she thought.

"Stop thinking that way," she scolded herself. "I am going to school happy, eager to finish my senior year."

She smiled as she remembered her crazy dream last night. She had been a beet, with short purple legs, and was waddling into the school cafeteria. Suddenly, a bunch of boys and girls, like crows, swooped down on her, screeching, "Her boyfriend left her. We can eat her up now."

Awake, Tabbie knew that wouldn't happen, but she felt uneasy.

She wondered if Dorcas was burrowing under blankets in her room.

Tabbie remembered the dramatic scene that Dorcas staged last night about returning to school.

"I don't think I'll go," she told Phoebe and her dad as each of them reached into their pockets and purse to find dollar bills for the twins' lunches.

"The meals are tasteless and classes are boring. I could teach most of them myself. I need to start college right now," Dorcas had said.

"Dorcas, you are going to classes, so stop saying you aren't!" Richard said firmly.

"You can always learn something, Dorcas," Phoebe said. "Pay attention, and then ask the teacher if you can go to the library, look up additional information, and write a report. You'll get an A plus in those courses."

"But I'm smarter than the teacher."

"You're bragging with no foundation to base it on," Richard said. "I know several of them, and they excelled in their classes at Dartmouth and University of Vermont."

As Tabbie listened to their conversation, she felt herself shrink inside, her anxiety returning. *Would Dorcas always set the tone for day or night?* She wondered.

The evening ended with Phoebe saying, "Dorcas, I want you to help Tabbie. Stop any gossiping and sit with her in the lunchroom if she's alone."

Dorcas walked over, kissed Tabbie's cheek, and said, "Sleep well. I'll help you tomorrow," and then she disappeared into her room.

XXXXX

At 7:00 a.m., Tabbie heard someone come into her room. She peeked out from under her blankets and saw Phoebe coming over to pull them off. Phoebe tickled her toes. "The radiator is on in the bathroom. Hurry and get dressed."

Every molecule in Tabbie wanted to stay in bed to avoid going to school without Thomas, but she remembered her new phrase: "I am strong without him." She kicked her legs to wake them, looked at the clothes she had laid on her chair last night—a lifeless gray pleated skirt, white blouse, and gray sweater—and said, "I must have been in a funk." She went to her closet and chose a robin's egg–blue skirt; she took out a flowered blouse and blue sweater from her bureau and went into the bathroom to dress.

Fifteen minutes later, Phoebe, Richard, Tabbie, and Dorcas were eating breakfast in the kitchen. Phoebe and Richard were the only ones talking.

"Do you know your schedule, girls?" Phoebe asked.

They nodded.

"What do you have for your elective?" Richard asked.

They nodded again, indicating that they weren't listening. Tabbie was repeating words of reassurance in her mind.

Dorcas glanced at her watch. "We've got to leave," she said, throwing Tabbie's backpack at her and heaving hers to her shoulder. They went outside and climbed into Phoebe's car.

Dorcas's mood changed from sleepiness to excitement. "I'm going to drop by your school, Aunt Phoebe, and ask the fourth-grade teacher if I can help her students produce *Pinocchio*. I met a little boy this summer who would be a perfect Pinocchio. Tabbie, you could play Giacomo. I'll help you learn the lines. We'll go over them so many times you'll say them in your sleep."

Tabbie stiffened. She imagined Dorcas's insistent and critical voice giving directions. Dorcas had little patience, and she would want her to act the part perfectly.

"Thanks, Dorcas," Tabbie answered. "It's going to take all my energy to focus in class. Please choose someone else."

Phoebe slowed the car down in front of the two-story stone high school. Dorcas climbed out, spotted Penelope, and ran over to her.

Tabbie backed out of the car slowly. *What will the students say when they see me without Thomas?* She wondered. *I don't care*, she decided, straightening her posture and walking toward the front door.

Her friend Janie came up, smiling. Janie had spent the summer with her grandmother and cousins in Minnesota.

"Did you have a good summer?" Janie asked.

"Until Thomas dumped me."

"I thought you were engaged?" Janie cocked her head.

"He changed his mind," Tabbie said as the school bell rang.

"I'm sorry," Janie said, hugging her. "I have to go to math now. Let's meet for lunch. I want to tell you about the cute boy I met over the summer. He said he'd write me. I want to tell you what we did in the cabin."

Tabbie nodded. Her first class was history; her dad was teaching it, which helped her get over her biting-nail nervousness.

Janie and Tabbie met for lunch in the cafeteria; they got trays with helpings of meat loaf, stiff whipped potatoes, and slushy green beans on them.

"It looks awful," Tabbie said, gagging.

"Let's toss it in the trash can," Jane said. "I've got some Ritz crackers in my pocket. Come on, we'll go outside to walk the track, and I'll tell you about Rick."

XXXXX

The next two weeks, Tabbie thought she caught glimpses of Thomas in the cafeteria, but it was always someone else. *Am I having a nervous breakdown?* she wondered. *No, any girl would act the same way*, she reassured herself. When she walked into the classroom, girls looked at her and whispered. Sarah, the president of Students Who Care Club, came up to her and asked if she was all right. Tabbie smiled and said, "Fine," but inside, she felt worn-out; she had used up her energy for the day.

XXXXX

At the end of September, maple leaves turned orange, red, and yellow.

Tabbie managed the first month of school with bravery. She had thought another boy might ask her for dates, but no one had. When she finished school in the afternoons, she walked over to Phoebe's elementary school and studied. At four o'clock, Phoebe gathered up her papers and Tabbie to take home. Dorcas stayed until six o'clock to help the fourth graders rehearse *Pinocchio*.

Tabbie walked into the house, laid her books on the kitchen counter, and reached for a slice of banana bread. She went into the living room, turned on the television, and stared; she felt alone. She rubbed her bare ring finger, and her broken dreams came back to her.

A dart shot through his chest. She wasn't going to marry Thomas. They wouldn't make love. She wouldn't be finding supper recipes from *The Joy of Cooking* that she had already bought.

She sat up and said to herself, "Life will be better without him. He's not trustworthy." She walked into the kitchen. "Can I help you fix supper, Aunt Phoebe? I'm ruminating over Thomas and want to cut him out of my mind. Maybe I can slice beets and substitute him for the vegetable."

"Here's a sharp knife and a cutting board," Phoebe said, joining Tabbie's game. "I'm heating up boiling water. You can dump him in there too."

Dorcas bounded in the door. She found Tabbie in the kitchen and grabbed her. "Tabbie, after my school kids act out *Pinocchio*, we are putting on *101 Dalmatians* winter semester. I want you to be a dog. All you have to do is bark. Can I count on you?"

"I don't think so."

"Tabbie, your life is so dull. It would liven you up," Dorcas said, shoving Tabbie's chest.

"Leave, Dorcas, she doesn't feel well," Phoebe said.

"She's been sick the entire month. I'm glad she's not contagious," Dorcas said, exiting.

"Aunt Phoebe, I know I'm not supposed to miss Thomas, but I do," Tabbie said, washing off the knife and putting it in the dish rack. "Sometime I feel like there's a big hole inside of me. I feel empty."

"Tabbie, Thomas didn't want to leave you. He figured he had to in order to get good grades. You are worth more than the stars and fireflies," Phoebe said, remembering when Tabbie was younger she and Dorcas used to capture fireflies and put them in a jar. Tabbie used to run over and tell Phoebe, "I got a star from heaven."

Phoebe leaned forward to look deep in Tabbie's eyes; their noses bumped. "Tabbie, many people love you. Have you talked to your dad about this?"

Tabbie shook her head.

"After supper, I want you to talk with him," Phoebe said.

XXXXX

After eating meat loaf, beets, corn bread and a crispy salad, Phoebe and Dorcas washed and dried the dishes while Richard and Tabbie walked down a small dirt road that tires of farmers' trucks had made as they drove giant bundles of harvested hay to their barns.

Tabbie looked over at her dad. "I know cows have to eat in the winter, but I miss the milkweed and black-eyed Susans that the farmers cut. If I were rich, I'd buy feed for their livestock and keep them out of our fields."

"Maybe you will be wealthy someday. You can publish your journals."

"Dad," she said, startled. "Those are private." She looked at him suspiciously. "You haven't read them, have you?"

"No, honey. I was teasing you."

Tabbie became quiet. She didn't know whether she was supposed to start the serious conversation or whether he was. She waited; Richard watched her.

"Your aunt says that you're not feeling well. Can you tell me about it?" he asked.

She hesitated. *How honest should I be?* she wondered. "Dad, going to school without Thomas is hard."

"Tabbie, do you want me to drive you over to University of Vermont to see him?"

She looked hopeful. *Would he see me?* she wondered. *Probably not. He might be hugging another girl already as sex hungry as he is.*

"What's your answer, Tabbie?" Richard asked.

"I don't think so, Dad. I'm going to discard him forever."

"Tabbie, how about riding to school with me in the mornings and we'll let Dorcas ride with Phoebe? We can brighten each other's spirits and swap some chunks of love to chew on each day. How does that sound to you?"

"Good, if Dorcas doesn't pitch a fit. She will probably insist that she join us."

"I won't let her," Richard said, taking her hand and walking back inside.

When Dorcas saw them, she said, "How do you rate one-to-one time with Dad? Do I have to catch the depression disease?"

"I'm here if you want to hang out with me, Dorcas. You never ask."

"How about now, Dad? You can listen to me read *Macbeth*."

They went into the living room, where Dorcas picked up her new copy that Kate had just mailed to her; it was the only item on the coffee table. "Dad, do you want to hear Mom's inscription?"

"I'd rather not," he said, sitting on the couch.

Dorcas started reading, "To my talented daughter Dorcas. Soon you will be one of the best actresses in the state, and I'll groom you to act Lady Macbeth in New York City.

Love, Mom."

Dorcas looked at her dad. "Do you think Kate can predict the future? Will I live and act in New York City?"

"As stubborn as you both are, there's a good chance it will happen."

"What percent?" she asked.

"Eighty percent," he said.

"What can I do to make it 100 percent?" she asked, sitting next to him.

"Give up getting the last word in," he said, standing up. "I love you, Dorcas. You're talented, smart, and unpredictable. Life is always an adventure." He leaned down and kissed the top of her head; her curly red hair tickled his nose, and he sneezed. "When is your next haircut?" he asked. "Use this." He handed her ten dollars, blew her a kiss, and went back to the kitchen.

CHAPTER 5

In August, Tabbie got her trunk from under her bed and began packing fall clothes into it—sweaters, long sleeve shirts, and jeans. She was going to her teacher's college on the weekend.

As she leaned over it, a cool fall breeze blew through the window onto her face; she shivered. "I'm leaving everyone I care about and who cares about me: Dad, who pumps love into me; Phoebe, who listens with her warm heart; Cindy, whose friendship builds my confidence."

Bess and Dorcas, she tossed aside. Dorcas's departing comment was "Anyone can get into the Vermont Teachers College. All you have to be able to do is spell and write sentences." Bess offered to let her take any fuzzy, purring cat from the shelter "When you're cold and lonely in your bed, your cat will cuddle beside you."

Dorcas would be leaving for college a week later. She had packed only two suitcases because Kate had already filled two bureau drawers with new clothes.

Tabbie pulled on a sweatshirt and warmed herself with phrases like "I'm smart enough to do well in my classes; I'm a leader now and will meet students easily." She picked up her journal and wrote,

"Dear Lord. Give me the courage and strength to leave my family and friend Janie and to start a successful year at college. Will I fit in with other students? Let my roommate be someone I can share feelings and study with. Let her not be like Dorcas. Should I date?"

She stopped writing and imagined a whole pond of handsome boys swimming after her; her dad said they would. She could see herself jump out of the water and run away. She returned to journaling. "No, I don't trust them. They start out kissing every inch of your face and ears and then move below the border."

She had gotten a surprise postcard from Thomas yesterday. It read, "Good luck at the Teacher's College. Sorry you won't be here at UVM. Thomas."

When Tabbie read it, she closed her eyes and breathed in deeply, wondering if she might detect Thomas's odor, but she didn't. She ripped the card into tiny pieces and threw it in the compost heap by the mudroom door.

As she finished packing her trunk, she heard a knock on the door and Phoebe's voice. "Are you ready? Cindy will be here at nine thirty to say good-bye." When Tabbie opened it, Phoebe handed her a small paper bag tied with a green-and-blue ribbon, the colors of her new college.

Tabbie opened it and pulled out a pair of green-and-blue wool socks that Phoebe had knit for her. "Wear them when you need courage, Tabbie. You'll feel God and me wrapped around you, whispering, 'Go forward.'"

"Thank you, Aunt Phoebe. Do I need to keep them in mothballs?"

"Not as long as you wear them. Mothballs are for summer when you put them away." Phoebe looked into the full trunk stuffed with warm sweaters, kneesocks, and skirts. Tabbie's down pillow lay on top enclosed in its pale-green pillowcase. Tabbie had used the pillow since childhood. When she put her head on it, she thought of happy times: playing games with her dad and listening to Aunt Phoebe read to her at night.

Before Tabbie closed her trunk, Phoebe handed her a new flowered pillowcase to replace the old one, saying, "You're starting a new life, Tabbie. Take this with you."

Tabbie thanked her. "I'll put it on when my other one gets dirty."

"We have an hour before Cindy arrives. Why don't you join your dad and me for a late breakfast?"

She nodded, and they walked into the kitchen together. Tabbie went over to her dad and kissed him on his cheek; she smelled the coffee on his breath and wondered, *Will I drink coffee at college to keep me alert at night? I hate the taste and odor. It's like swallowing dirt and smelling trash.* She poured herself orange juice and sat down with them.

"How did you sleep, Tabbie?" Phoebe asked.

"Fair."

"How do you feel about leaving today?" Richard asked.

"I'm nervous, but I'm ready. I'm going to miss both of you. Will you call me on Sundays?"

"We certainly will," Phoebe said. "Remember your beauty and gentleness."

Tabbie hesitated before she made her next remark, then she continued, "What if I meet a bully like Dorcas?"

Richard said, "Ignore him or her and walk away."

"What if he or she comes after me?"

"Find a strong boy who will protect you," Richard said.

"I'm not dating the first semester," she reminded him.

Phoebe and Richard got up to hug her. They were all wiping tears from their eyes. "The house will be lonely without you," Richard said.

"Remember that God and I will be praying for you," Phoebe said. She handed Tabbie a blue-and-green journal. "Keep writing, Tabbie, and if you have time, send me a postcard." Phoebe handed her five stamped and addressed cards.

At nine thirty, Cindy arrived, and she and Richard peeked into Tabbie's room, where she was taking sheets off her bed to wash and folding blankets.

"Can we come in?" Cindy asked.

Tabbie turned; she looked pretty in a pair of jeans and a blue shirt.

Cindy hugged her and handed her a package wrapped in pink tissue paper. "It's for our future."

Tabbie pulled out a book whose title was *Stories of Inner City Teachers*.

"Thank you, Cindy. You can read it after me."

"I'm next." Richard gave Tabbie an envelope. He apologized as she opened it. "I didn't know what to pick out for you." She pulled out a gift certificate for fifty dollars for Mabel's clothing store in Glennsboro.

"Oh, Dad, thank you. I'll see what the kids in college are wearing and buy the same."

"Remember that you don't have to match them. You are an individual," Cindy said. "And a lovely, smart one at that."

Tabbie slipped the new journal in the side of her trunk and closed it. Richard and Cindy carried it out and loaded it in the back of Phoebe's car.

Dorcas, who had spent the night at Bess's house, came running across the lawn while Bess followed more slowly. Dorcas gave Tabbie a small embrace. "Good-bye, sister. Do well. Don't let anyone crush your emotions. Be careful with boys, and don't choose anyone to date until I check them out."

Bess said, "If you want me to drive over to your campus when you're taking a psychology class and discussing pets that soothe naughty children, I'll bring my cat and prodigy, Monkey Do, over."

Tabbie half-listened to their farewells; she didn't want to cry and puncture her confidence. "Thank you, Dorcas. I hope you like your college. Bess, thank you for offering that. I'll keep it in mind." Then she and Phoebe climbed into the car. Everyone waved, and Phoebe honked as she drove off.

XXXXX

After an hour and a half of driving, Phoebe arrived at the front gate of the campus. She stopped the car and turned to Tabbie. "Are you ready?" She smiled.

Tabbie smiled softly back. "I'm ready."

Phoebe handed her a campus map. "Please help me find Deacon Hall."

"It looks like it's down McCall Street. We're on that now," Tabbie said.

Phoebe drove down the street and stopped in front of a four-tory, brick building with red, blue, and yellow balloons waving in the breeze. Tabbie breathed in deeply. *There's nothing to fear*, she told herself.

Phoebe parked in front of the dorm, and she and Tabbie removed blankets, pillows, and laundry bags filled with jackets and shoes from the car. Indoor, they dropped them at the bottom of the stairs.

"I don't think I can climb the three flights of stairs to your room, Tabbie," Phoebe apologized.

They heard a voice behind them say, "Dad, we can use the elevator." A father and daughter were carrying suitcases, duffel bags, and a trunk to an elv bevator.

Phoebe walked over and introduced herself. "I'm Phoebe Thorndike, and my grandniece, Tabbie, is going to be a freshman." Phoebe motioned Tabbie forward.

"I'm Richard Billingsley, and my daughter Wendy is a freshman also."

Smiling, Wendy shook Phoebe's hand and Tabbie's. "What room are you in?" Wendy asked Tabbie. She was Tabbie's height, with wavy black hair, and was already wearing a blue-and-green sweatshirt that had "Vermont Teachers College" printed on it.

"In 315. How about you?" Tabbie asked.

Wendy said, "215. I'm right below you."

Mr. Billingsley said, "After we get Wendy's load up, I'd be happy to help you."

"We have a heavy trunk in the car. I'd appreciate that," Phoebe said. She wondered where Wendy's mother was. Should she ask while they were waiting for the elevator? She had learned to be direct as principal of Bradberry Elementary School. "Where's your mother, Wendy?"

"She's enrolling my twin sister at University of Vermont today."

"Tabbie has a twin sister also. She has a passion for acting and is going to Hepburn College in Hampton. You and Tabbie will have a lot to talk about."

The elevator arrived, and Mr. Billingsley stuck his foot in the door so it wouldn't close without their load. "We'll be down in a moment, and then you can use it," he said.

In ten minutes, the Billingsleys returned. "The rooms are small, and so are the closets. I don't know how Wendy is going to fit everything in," Mr. Billingsley said, shaking his head. "Where is your car? I'll bring the trunk in."

"I parked it in front," Phoebe replied. "If you wait, I'll help you."

"Wendy and I can get it. You take your load up."

"Thanks," Phoebe said. She and Tabbie loaded their bags and stuffed pillowcases into the dark elevator. The light had burned out. Tabbie pushed three. It clanked and rattled. Tabbie said, "I don't like this noise. It doesn't sound safe. I'm going to climb the stairs from now on."

"Good. It will give you strong legs. Isn't that nice that you and Wendy can share twin stories?"

"But mine aren't very good," Tabbie said.

"Hers might be worse," Phoebe said.

When they got out, they found room 315 down the hall.

"Use your key," Phoebe said. The school had sent Tabbie a key along with instructions about moving in and who her roommate would be.

As Tabbie was getting it from her purse, the door opened. A cute girl with curly blond hair hugged Tabbie. She said in an energetic and friendly way, "Hi, Tabbie. I'm Suzie. I'm so excited that we're going to be roommates. We're going to love being independent and away from home. We're going to have good teachers, meet cute boys, and help each other through crushes and rejections."

Tabbie stiffened, thinking, *This won't work. I won't be spunky enough for Suzie. She'll be bored with me and ask for another roommate.* Then Tabbie reminded herself of her good qualities, and she returned Suzie's hug.

"We're going to be best friends and have a good time," Suzie said. "Let me help you unpack. I've taken the desk, and I left the table with a drawer for you. You've got the bed and the closet with shelves on the left side. There's not room for all our clothes. I'm keeping my trunk at the end of my bed and stuffing sweaters, wool socks, and hats in there. It's supposed to be a cold winter. Do you have a trunk?"

"Another student's father is bringing it up," Phoebe said. "I think I'll leave. You two are already like sisters."

"Not sisters," Tabbie corrected her. She turned to Suzie. 'I've got a disagreeable twin."

"We can be cherry sizzlers that stick to each other," Suzie said. She reached in her pants pocket and pulled apart two rubbery candy sticks. "Would you like one?" she asked Phoebe.

"No, thanks, I'd lose my fillings." Phoebe hugged Tabbie. "I'll write you tonight," she said, leaving.

XXXXX

The first month, Tabbie felt sad and missed the familiar rhythms of home: Phoebe listening and encouraging her; Cindy's energy, enthusiasm, and plans for Project Teach; and her dad's love. She wrote postcards each day, saying something positive so they wouldn't worry about her. When she went to her mailbox, she found letters from Phoebe daily and Cindy or her dad on alternating days.

In the last part of October, she got one signed by both Cindy and her Dad.

Dear Tabbie,

We've decided to marry. We share a lot—our love for you and Dorcas, for each other, and our hiking.

We will marry the day before Thanksgiving in a small family gathering at the Congregational Church in Bradberry. Our wedding meal will be on

Thanksgiving. Our love is creating positive energy, and new plans are popping out everywhere. Can't wait to tell you about them. We love you.

Dad and Cindy

Thanksgiving was six weeks away. Tabbie hadn't heard from Dorcas since the start of college. She was curious how Dorcas was doing. Tabbie asked Suzie to stand beside her as she dialed Kate's number. Phoebe had told her that Dorcas and her roommate usually ate supper at Kate's.

"Hello, Kate's acting studio and café," Kate answered.

Tabbie squeezed Suzie's hand for strength. "How are you, Kate? It's Tabbie. Is Dorcas there?"

"Yes. I'll get her," Kate said. "But first tell me how you like your college. Are the courses hard? Are your friends intelligent? Is there a drama department?"

"Those are a lot of questions, Kate. I like college and my friends. There isn't a drama department, but there are several courses about plays and playwrights."

"Make sure you take them, Tabbie, so you can communicate with your sister. She has already tried out for a play, *Macbeth*, and got the part of Lady Macbeth.

We will be putting it on the first week of December. I hope you will come and see it."

"I don't have a car, but maybe Phoebe or Dad and Cindy can bring me over."

"You can leave Cindy at home. Here's Dorcas."

"Tabbie!" Dorcas's voice was actressy. "How is my sister doing at her teacher's college? Are you ready to teach me how to behave? I may never learn since I'm acting the part of Lady Macbeth, who is selfish, cruel, and murderous. I promise I will never murder you, Tabbie."

"Thank you, Dorcas. Did you get the note from Dad and Cindy?"

"I did," Dorcas answered, as if she wasn't much interested.

"Do you like Hepburn?"

"It's scrumptious. I read and act plays twenty-four hours a day. Are you managing to stay at the teacher's college? No homesickness, faints, or failures?"

"I have a wonderful roommate who helps me study math, and I help her with English. All is going well." There was a pause. "I've got to go. I'm meeting her in five minutes. Good-bye." Tabbie hung up the phone.

"Was she nice to you?" Suzie asked.

"She didn't have time to topple me over," Tabbie said.

XXXXX

The last part of October was windy; colored maple leaves fell off the tree branches into crispy, crunchy piles on the ground. Suzie and Tabbie had joined the college hiking club. On weekends, they gathered with eight other students to walk on Coosa Trail, along a creek, and up to the top of the mountain.

One Saturday, as they started their hike, a car honked, and a young man with short black hair jumped out, yelling, "Stop. Is Tabbie Thorndike there?"

Tabbie's heart stopped; she gasped for breath and started coughing. She leaned into Suzie, who was wearing a dark-brown flannel shirt. "That's Thomas, the boy I dated in high school," she whispered. Her mind whipped around ways to avoid him. *I can run and hide or yell to the group that he's a city boy who pollutes the forests.* But it was too late. Thomas was pulling at her sleeve, plucking her from the group.

"Tabbie, don't pretend that you don't know me. I've driven all the way from University of Vermont to see you."

"I didn't ask you to," she whispered back.

"Skip the hike. Stay back and visit with me." Thomas turned to the leader. "I'm an old friend of hers. You go on, and she'll join you next time."

Tabbie knew she had the strength to say no to Thomas. She had visualized this scene many times when she first came to college. She would say, "Leave. My love for you is over." But seeing his soft tan face, blue eyes, and dimples and feeling his hand on her sleeve made her want to hold back from the hike and visit with him. She imagined hearing Phoebe's and her dad's voices, warning her. "Insist that he leave right away."

Suzie whispered, "Don't give in, Tabbie. Tell him to leave."

Tabbie stared at her. "He's a friend, Suzie. I'll stay and visit with him."

"Don't let him weave a spell, "she warned.

"I'll talk, and that's all." Tabbie stepped out of the line. The hikers climbed down the hill to the head of the trail while Tabbie sent a prayer to God, Phoebe, Cindy, and her dad. *Keep me strong.*

She looked at Thomas but was unable to return his smile. "We can go to a swinging branch that I've just discovered and look across the valley," she suggested, walking slowly.

Thomas stopped her. "I've got our kissing blanket in the car. Let's find a quiet place and lie down together."

Tabbie pulled away. "Thomas, you're visiting my campus, and you'll follow my rules. Rule number 1: no touching. Number 2: the visit lasts thirty minutes. Number 3: topics will be related to school, not love."

When they sat on the branch, Tabbie kept her body muscles tight and her stomach sucked in. When she loosened them, she could feel the sexual tingling rush through her. She started the conversation. "How are you doing in your pre-med classes?"

He ignored her question. "I'm sorry that I broke up with you. I'm doing better than I thought I would, and I'd like to restart our relationship."

"Thomas, you are talking about a topic that's off limits." Tabbie felt tears forming inside. *Switch to anger*, she told herself. Suzie had told her that feeling mad was a natural feeling, just like feeling sad, scared, and happy. They had been practicing angry phrases that she could use. She tried to release one now: "I am angry at you for leaving me so suddenly. I will never date you again." After she said that, she returned to a school question. "Have you dissected a person yet?"

Thomas looked hurt and confused. "Tabbie, don't you love me?" he asked, moving close to her. "We have the opportunity to feel it again."

Don't give in, Tabbie told herself. She imagined her supporters echoing the words "Don't give in." "Thomas, I'm afraid you'll have to leave now. You broke the rules."

He grabbed her, squeezed her in his arms, and kissed her.

For an instant, Tabbie felt her old longing. But she leaped up. "Go away, Thomas. Our love is over." She walked along the path that led to her dorm.

Thomas ran after her and twirled her around. "Think about what you're doing, Tabbie. You won't ever know what it's like to love me intimately."

Tabbie stared at him. She could be like Dorcas and say, "I don't give a damn," or she could be like Suzie and say, "You had a chance and bungled it. Please don't come again."

"I brought you a gift, Tabbie. Open it, and maybe you'll change your mind." He handed her a flat package wrapped in blue-and-green paper, her favorite colors.

"Thank you Thomas. I'll take it back to my room."

"No, Tabbie, please do it now," he urged, tearing the paper off himself. He handed her a framed eight-by-ten photograph of the two of them kissing in front of Bradberry falls. He beamed at her. "Remember when that other couple offered to take this photo and we snapped one of them kissing?" His smile was as large as a two-year-old boy's when his mother offered him a lollipop. "I bet they're still in love. Can't you go back to loving me?"

Tabbie looked at him; her heart felt sad when she answered, "No, Thomas. I have to leave. Good-bye and good luck." She turned and walked down the path that went to her dorm, moving aside to let several couples pass. When she got back to her dorm room, she couldn't wait to share her success with Suzie.

XXXXX

A day before Thanksgiving, Richard's and Cindy's families and friends gathered at the Congregational Church at 11:00 a.m. Phoebe had ordered white roses that she put on one side of the altar. Bess put white carnations on the other side. As the organist played the wedding march on a hundred-year-old organ, Cindy walked down the aisle in a simple white percale dress with flowers embroidered on the scoop-necked top. She stood beside Richard at the altar. He was wearing a tan suit with a blue shirt and tie that Cindy had chosen for him.

Pastor Tate, dressed in a simple black robe, looked out at the small group gathered in the pews. Cindy's parents and her two brothers sat on one side of the church. Phoebe, Bess, Tabbie, and Dorcas sat on the other side. Several of Cindy's teacher-friends attended also.

Pastor Tate asked, "Do all of you, who are gathered here together, bless this union?"

Everyone said, "We do."

"Then we'll continue with the ceremony."

After they exchanged vows, Richard and Cindy pledged love to each other, kissed, and walked down the aisle as everyone clapped. Friends gathered in the fellowship hall for punch, pumpkin pies, and muffins. This gave Richard's family the opportunity to meet Cindy's parents, who were both teachers in Boston. Tabbie talked to them about plans for Project Teach in New York City.

"Are you going to join them?" Cindy's father asked Dorcas.

"I'll be acting in New York City," she said.

At 1:00 p.m., Cindy and Richard drove off in their car, decorated with streamers and balloons, to spend their honeymoon night at the Four Columns Inn in Forsyth.

Dorcas rode home with Bess and Tabbie with Phoebe. "Can we take the long road home?" she asked. "I want to talk to you about a boy I've met. His name is Eric, and he's in my hiking group. He's smart, handsome, and delicious. He seems to like me. I don't know what to do. Shall I pay attention to him? I'm not sure I want to fall in love again. I think Thomas spooked me. Can I be friends with a boy and not start kissing?"

Phoebe said, "I can try to answer that, but it will be a thirty-years-ago response. Maybe Cindy and your dad can share more recent ideas with you. Thirty years ago, when I was dating my fiancé Stanley, we kissed, laughed, hiked, and pledged loyalty to each other. When the logger truck hit and killed him, we lost our chance to consummate our love. Our relationship ended." She began to cry.

Tabbie squeezed her arm. "How sad that he was killed. How different your life would have been if you had married. I hope that we have brought you some happiness."

"Of course you have, probably more than if Stanley and I were together."

"Is it hard to go to weddings, Aunt Phoebe?" Tabbie asked.

"No, I pray for the joy of the couple. When you marry, I'll be like a jumping frog squealing and peeping."

CHAPTER 6

At 11:00 a.m., on a snowy morning, Richard and Cindy returned from their one-night honeymoon to help prepare Thanksgiving dinner. Tabbie greeted them at the door and handed them a card. Cindy opened it and read, "Welcome to our bride and groom. We are giving you a no-work Thanksgiving meal. Sit, hug, and whisper until we call you to the table. Love, Tabbie and Phoebe."

Cindy hugged Tabbie. "What about the cranberry oatmeal dish I planned to make?"

"I've already cooked it, mashed the potatoes, and fixed the green beans. Aunt Phoebe stuffed and cooked the turkey and mixed her famous gravy. Aunt Bess is bringing her chocolate cake."

"What did Dorcas do?" Richard asked, anticipating "Nothing" for an answer.

"She set the table and created place cards," Phoebe said.

"Those aren't edible," Richard answered. "She keeps talking about the tapas she makes at her mother's. I guess we're too country for those."

"Let's look at our bedroom," Cindy said, taking Richard's hand and going into his room, which was off the dining room. He had cleaned out his closet and bureau drawers so Cindy could share the space. Cindy was delighted with the sweet angelic smell of roses and white lilies in a vase on the bureau when they walked in.

Cindy breathed in deeply. "I'm going to sleep with you and dream of our pine tree path where we put our sleeping bag over the summer. Do you remember the warm night when we slept under the stars until three a.m.? When we realized the time, we picked up our bag and hurried home, feeling guilty. Now we can do that any or every night, and we're legitimate." She kissed him.

"It might be the only privacy we get," Richard said, leaning Cindy into a gentle backbend and kissing her.

Someone knocked on the door. Tabbie called through the wood, "Dinner is ready. Bess just arrived with buttered beets and her chocolate cake."

Cindy took Richard's hand, and they walked through the dining room into the kitchen "How can I help?" She sniffed at the oven door. "The turkey smells yummy and the cranberry casserole tart. I love Thanksgiving." She hugged Phoebe. "Growing up, the holiday at our home was bedlam. My brothers would reach across the table for whatever they wanted. Elbows were always bumping salt-and-pepper shakers into the cranberry dressing. They never helped in the kitchen. If they offered, they broke plates, so it was better that they went to their rooms to play."

"We had those days too—spilled milk, burns and stains from scalding coffee, and dropped chocolate cake on the floor," Phoebe said. "Could you help me carry the food into the dining room, and, Richard, could you carve the turkey?"

As if on cue, Dorcas and Bess appeared. Dorcas wore an orange V-necked sweater and a long black skirt.

"Everyone, find your place cards and sit down," Phoebe instructed.

"Are my beets on the table?" Bess asked, looking around.

"Next to the mashed potatoes." Tabbie pointed.

"Richard, will you say grace, please?" Phoebe asked.

They bowed their heads. "God, thank you for this opportunity to share Thanksgiving together. Thank you for Cindy's and my marriage and for our family. God bless all of us as we work to help others. Amen."

As they picked up their forks, Dorcas spoke, "I tried out for *Macbeth* and got the leading part of Lady Macbeth. I remember what you said, Aunt Phoebe: 'Share the stage, Dorcas, don't steal it.' I'm better at that now."

They heard the front door open. Kate and her husband, Ronald, burst into the dining room. "Happy Thanksgiving, I've brought dessert," Kate called out. She was wearing a red velvet dress. Ronald, who was dressed in a pale-orange shirt and leather jacket, reluctantly followed.

Tabbie's heart fell to her toes. Phoebe hadn't told her that Kate was coming.

Phoebe looked stunned. "What brings you here?" she asked, not knowing what else to say.

Dorcas smiled. "Mother, I invited you, but you said you were eating at home."

"I'm not sure you're wanted here," Bess said.

Cindy whispered to Richard, "This is embarrassing."

Kate handed Richard a bottle of champagne. "I hope you and your wife will be happy." She looked over at Tabbie. "I hear you've chosen your major, Tabbie. Teaching will suit you well. You know more than second graders."

Tabbie wasn't sure how to answer that but breathed in deeply and replied in a strong voice, "I like teaching. Cindy and I have plans to start a program, Project Teach. We're going to New York City to help inner-city children."

Phoebe, the epitome of politeness, got up to add two more place settings at the table.

Kate continued to talk. "Richard, I hope that you can make your marriage work. It seems Cindy is more docile than I was. I haven't heard her say much. I was feisty and stubborn. It takes someone like Ronald to tame me."

"I wonder how he has survived," Richard said, a partial stab.

"I'll answer him, darling," Kate said, patting Ronald's arm. "First of all, he finds me clever and charming. Next, he puts me in charge of our weekly calendar. I decide when we go out to eat and where. Doesn't he look content?"

"Who pays the bills?" Bess asked.

Kate pointed to him. "He's the director of the drama department, and his salary is higher than mine. How big is yours, Richard?"

"I don't have to tell you, Kate. In fact, your presence at our Thanksgiving and wedding meal is growing very annoying." Richard stood up. "You can both leave now."

Cindy smiled; she was proud of Richard's boldness and bravery.

"The bride and groom seem to be of one accord," Phoebe said, standing. "I will fix you two plates to go."

"Dad, where is your charity? Tell them they can stay and eat," Dorcas said.

"It's all right, Dorcas. A couple from the drama department invited us for a late Thanksgiving meal. I think the conversation will be more stimulating," Kate said, getting up to go."

As she shut the front door, Tabbie surprised everyone by saying, "I wonder how Shakespeare would end this play?"

XXXXX

Sunday, after Thanksgiving, Cindy and Richard took Tabbie back to college. She sat in the back seat, leaning forward to talk about boys. "Eric, who is a freshman, is cute, quiet, and sweet like you, Dad. He has brown eyes the color of chestnut and hair the same color. His voice is slow and patient, and he waits for me to talk before he does. When he looks at me, his eyes smile. I think he likes me because he follows me to the library and asks if he can help me with math."

"Pick him, Tabbie. You'll like him more and more as he does kind things for you," Cindy said.

"Wait, Cindy, she hasn't told us about all her suitors," Richard said.

"Another boy named Ricardo seems to like me also. He's cute, about my height, has black hair, a dark complexion, and brown eyes that coax me to follow him. He's from Lima, Peru. His parents also have a home in Miami. His dad owns a sugarcane plantation, and they are wealthy."

"Have you asked him about the *barriadas* and how the poor people live?" Cindy asked.

"Yes, he said that some of his father's workers live there but he has never visited them. The people in *barriadas* are sick with contagious diseases."

Tabbie was going to ask Cindy and her dad which boy she should date, but she stopped herself. *I'm independent now and have to make my own decisions,* she thought. *Suzie and I can debate it all day and night, or I can throw a coin—heads Ricardo and tails Eric.*

As they pulled up to the curb at the dorm, they saw Suzie was waiting for them. Eric was on one side of her and Ricardo on the other.

When Tabbie got out of the car, Eric approached her with two math sheets. "I've copied your next assignment and made some practice sheets for us to go over," he said, handing them to her.

"Thank you, Eric."

Ricardo came forward and handed her a red rose. "A beautiful flower for a beautiful girl." He kissed her cheek.

Tabbie took the rose and breathed in its sweetness. "Gracias, Ricardo."

A few awkward moments of silence followed. Her dad walked up. "Can I meet these boys, Tabbie?"

"Ricardo, Eric, this is my dad, Richard Thorndike, and my stepmom, Cindy."

Richard shook their hands. Cindy smiled and said, "Buenos dias."

"Habla Española, senora?" Ricardo said. "Me gusto su hija."

"Gracias," Cindy answered.

Eric and Richard talked about teaching school.

"In high school I tutored students in math," Eric said.

After brief conversations, the two boys waved and walked off in different directions.

Richard carried Tabbie's suitcase into the dorm with Suzie and Tabbie following. "They both want to date her," Suzie whispered to Cindy.

"Ricardo can teach me Spanish," Tabbie said.

"He has an 'I'm going to conquer you' look," Suzie said.

"It's called *machismo*," Tabbie answered. "Most men from Latin America have it."

"I'd watch out for him," she said.

"Listen to Suzie, Tabbie," Cindy said. "What do you think, Richard?"

"I liked Eric, but I'm a gringo."

Tabbie hugged them both. "Thank you for bringing me back."

XXXXX

Over the next month, Eric and Ricardo pursued Tabbie. Eric sought her out in the library and tutored her in math. They skied together at Mt. Snow; he brought tuna sandwiches that he made at home and a thermos of coffee. He refused to spend four dollars for a hot dog and three dollars for coffee at the concession stand.

Tabbie liked his thoughtfulness and enjoyed skiing, skating, and snowshoeing with him. She smiled at his thriftiness. *He's a good saver, and we'll never go broke.* Although she tried not to think of marriage, she did. Eric would make a good husband, responsible and hard-working. His plan to go to graduate school to become a principal was ambitious. Then she moved from the practical to the emotional. *Eric looks at me in a romantic way, our eyes lock, our lips quiver. We walk holding hands; he squeezes mine hard, and we become one.*

Suzie was coaching Eric on ways to court Tabbie. When she suggested a three-course meal at the steak house, he said, "No, she likes the french fries at McDonald's."

Ricardo kept calling Tabbie for dates. "Por favor, mi amor, vengo con migo. Mi corazon es caliente. Nos besamos." Please, my friend, come with me. My heart is hot. We kiss.

"Quiero estudio espanol con tigo en el biblioteca," Tabbie replied. I want to study Spanish with you in the library.

"Pero, yo tengo el vino, las floras y un regalo del Peru para tigo. Tu es mi mujer." But I have wine, flowers, and a present from Peru for you. You are my woman.

As Tabbie translated his words, she could feel herself withdraw. She didn't want to be a conquered woman so he could boast of his heightened machismo with his friends.

She practiced her phrase. "I'm sorry I can't date you." Yo tiengo dolor que no puedo feche tigo.

The next time he called, she spoke those words twice.

He replied, "Me corazon tiene dolor. Adios mi mujera linda." My heart has sadness. Good-bye, my pretty woman.

Tabbie was thrilled that she had chosen Eric as her boyfriend. On Friday night, he invited her to eat at McDonald's and go to a movie. "I've got something exciting to tell you, Eric," she told him.

"Did you get an A on your math test?" he asked in a congratulatory tone.

"No. I'll tell you when you get here. Hurry," she said, hanging up the phone.

In five minutes, he appeared in front of her dorm. She had been looking out the window and flew down the three flights of stairs to meet him in the hallway. They kissed briefly and walked hand in hand to the car. Parking was limited to fifteen minutes in front of the dorm.

"Let's go to the school parking lot. I want to excite you with some news," Tabbie said

"We have five minutes, or we'll be late to the movie."

As he drove slowly to the lot, complying with the campus speed limit of ten miles per hour, she began, "I've told Ricardo to go away, that I was your girl. I told him that you don't like opposition."

As he entered the dark, empty lot, he coughed. "I like you very much, Tabbie. In fact, I could easily fall in love with you, but it's too early. I promised myself that I would not date a girl seriously until junior year. My mother bewitched my father the second semester of freshman year. They married and had me seven months later. Both my mother and father dropped out of college to work to pay bills. They finished college in their thirties, which was difficult, but they were persistent."

As Tabbie listened to Eric talk, a veil dropped down over her eyes and she saw Thomas. She heard double voices in her ears; one was Thomas's. She tried to look directly at Eric, indicating interest in what he was saying and showing no emotion. "Eric, I think we can let our relationship roll naturally. We can decide when to slow it down, as if we are riding bikes down a hill and decide to apply the brakes."

"I don't know if we can resist getting tangled in each other's bodies. I'm the male and should set the limits, but I'm not sure I have the willpower."

"Don't worry, Eric, I know how to keep you from tangling me up. I've had plenty of practice preventing my twin sister, Dorcas, from capturing me in her web."

He thought for a minute. His face brightened. "I have a plan. I will ask my friend Ray and his girlfriend, Rachel, to ride with us to the movies, restaurants, and to Mt. Snow. That way, we won't be alone. We won't be tempted."

"What if they want to be alone!" she said, alarmed at his plan.

"I hadn't thought of that," he said, scratching his head.

"Let's skip dinner and a movie tonight," Tabbie said. "Please take me back to the dorm. I've got an English test on Monday and need to study."

"I'm taking the same test and will probably fail it if you don't help me review. Let's change our plans and go to the library, where you can tutor me."

"Not tonight, Eric. I've got to think over our conversation."

As he pulled his car up to the curb, Tabbie jumped out. "See you Monday in English class." She waved.

When she got back to her room, she saw Suzie was studying for her science exam.

Tabbie ran over to her, pulled up a chair, and reached for her hands. She started crying.

"What's wrong?" Suzie asked, squeezing her hands.

"Suzie, I think Eric is breaking up with me. He says he doesn't have time for me. He doesn't want to date seriously. What shall I do? I hope I don't collapse the way I did when Thomas broke up with me."

"I'll keep that from happening, Tabbie," Suzie said, moving onto the chair that Tabbie was sitting in. "Maybe that's a good idea, Tabbie. The point of freshman and sophomore year is to become independent and wise on our own. I'm afraid you'll grow too dependent on Eric."

"I think you're right. I'll tell him that after our English exam on Monday."

"I'm here to give you strength," Suzie said, hugging her.

"Thanks, friend, sister, and cherry sizzler." Tabbie changed into pajamas and climbed into bed; she pulled open the drawer in her bedside table and took out her journal.

Dear Lord,

I've missed the whole purpose of college. I came here to find a boyfriend to replace Thomas. Now I see more clearly that college is for studying. When do I fall in love, in junior year? Is that when boys give girls engagement rings? She rubbed her ring finger and was glad that Thomas hadn't placed a ring there. I'm confused, Lord.

Please give me some answers while I sleep.

Love,

Tabbie

On Monday, after their English exam, Tabbie and Eric walked out of the classroom together.

"Did you think it was difficult, Eric?" Tabbie asked.

"A sizzler," he said. "I would have done better if you had shown me the main themes to study."

"Eric, I've thought about our talk, Friday night. I also want to focus on studying this year. When I graduate, I plan to go to Peru with my dad's wife, Cindy. We are going to teach in the *barriados*."

As she talked, her eyes watered. She was giving up what she wanted most. She breathed in and smiled, feeling proud of herself; she had the courage to say no.

Eric smiled also. "We've come up with the same decision. Do you want me to continue helping you with math?"

"No. My roommate, Suzie, has a friend who is good at math."

He hesitated and then asked, "Who is that?"

"A boy named Samuel."

"I think you're making a mistake, Tabbie. I know Samuel, and he makes stupid mistakes on his tests." He hesitated. "Choose me, Tabbie. We can sit beside each other as friends."

Be strong, Tabbie, she told herself. "No, Eric. I've already set up a session with him."

"I don't have anything to worry about. He's a nerd," Eric said.

Looking at each other with regret and longing, they shook hands.

"Good-bye. Thank you for your help, Eric. So far, I have a C in algebra. I would be failing if it weren't for you."

"Good-bye, Tabbie," he said, giving her a quick hug. "Good luck in your plans to go to Peru. You'll be good and patient with the kids."

Each turned and walked in a different direction.

CHAPTER 7

By the end of sophomore year, Tabbie's math grades had risen to a B-plus. Samuel's twice-a-week tutoring had helped her twist numbers more skillfully.

Tabbie's beauty and kindness bewitched Samuel. He let his hair grow, dyed it brown to match hers, and wore green and blue clothes, knowing those were her favorite colors. One night, after studying between the library stacks on the third floor together, he got down on his knees to pledge his love to her.

"Would you consider marrying me? I'd make a wonderful husband," he asked, kissing her hand.

"I'm sorry, I can't. I've pledged myself to someone else," she said, standing up.

"Do I know the person?" he asked. "I'm ready to duel for you." He formed his body in a fencing position, extending his right hand forward.

"Samuel, you are my tutor. We are not going to date," she said, stuffing her math papers and book in her bag and heading for the stairs. On her way out, she saw Eric sitting at a study table, his chair pushed up close to a pretty blond girl whom she didn't recognize. He was erasing some numbers on a sheet of paper. "Recalculate that problem, Jenny. The answer should be 100."

Jenny gazed up at him with adoration. "How did you get so smart, Eric?"

As Tabbie passed them, she decided to drop her books; they crashed on the floor as if they were toy trains colliding into each other.

Without looking up, he said with annoyance, "Shhh. The library is a place of silence, not noise."

"Sorry," Tabbie said. "I know you. We used to date."

Jenny looked up at Tabbie, placed her hand over Eric's, and said, "He's my tutor. We meet here every night."

Eric looked up, his face tuning red as a sunset. He stood and shook Tabbie's hand.

"Is that how you greet a previous girlfriend?" she asked, hoping to embarrass him. "I think we left some things unsaid the last time we met. Let's meet in the cafeteria for lunch tomorrow." She whispered the time in Eric's ear so Jenny wouldn't hear.

Eric smiled and nodded.

Tabbie waved and walked into a spring evening.

XXXXX

The next day, when Tabbie met Eric, he kissed her cheek.

"I've saved a seat for us in the corner. It's quieter there. Jay is sitting on top of the table to keep other students away." They looked over and saw Jay waving. "Let's hurry through the line. He's got to go to class."

As Tabbie put a bacon-lettuce-and-tomato sandwich and cherry Jell-O on her tray, Eric loaded his with fried chicken, mashed potatoes, peas, and two pieces of chocolate cake. When they sat, they found that the noise around them was louder than a stadium full of footfall fans. He yelled, "You're eating thin, Tabbie. Do you want a piece of cake?"

She shook her head. "A girl has to be thin as a straw to keep boys chasing her. You're eating fat."

"I lost weight not seeing you much this year," he said, turning his mouth down.

She stared at him, at his perfectly chiseled face, brown eyes, and brown hair. *I still love him*, she thought. She prayed for courage and clarity. "Let's talk about our relationship, Eric. You start first."

"Lots of kissing, parking in the car, and dancing nude," he said.

"Eric, I'm serious. I've missed you. I'd like to go out again with some rules. Nod if you agree."

He tilted his head, scratching it. "What are they?"

"We will only date each other."

He nodded.

"We can whisper words of love, even look up poems, like Browning's, and read them to each other, but we aren't going to have sex. Can you go along with that?"

"I'll try my hardest," he said, feeding her a piece of cake.

XXXXX

Summer passed quickly. Eric worked in his uncle's lumber mill, and Tabbie helped Cindy teach summer school.

Dorcas stayed with her mom, Kate, at Hepburn College, helping put on plays.

Tabbie started her junior year on the second week of September. Packing seemed routine now. Shoes went to the bottom of her trunk; underwear, bras, and sweaters on the second tier; and skirts, pants, and jewelry on the top layer along with her new red journal. She chose that color because she hoped this would be a year of love for her and Eric.

Phoebe drove her to the campus, and they arrived at noon. Eric was standing in front of the dorm.

"He's punctual," Phoebe said. "Your dad called him to ask if he would help us unload the trunk."

Tabbie opened the window to greet him, and she almost fell out. "Eric, welcome back to junior year. I'm excited about it. Are you?"

He nodded. "We're taking a lot of the same classes since we're both majoring in education. Who is going to help whom?"

Tabbie wanted to say something clever. "Sometimes you'll be on top. Other times I'll be on top." She blushed. That could refer to lovemaking, she thought, reprimanding herself. *This year is about studying and getting Bs, not getting hickeys.*

The trunk knocked and banged as Eric dragged it to the third floor. Tabbie and Phoebe rode the elevator and met him at the top of the stairs.

"Thanks, Muscle Man," Tabbie said, leaning over to kiss him.

"Can I peck your cheek?" Phoebe asked, leaning over.

"Only if we don't start dating," Eric joked, looking over at Tabbie and smiling.

Suzie greeted them at the door. "You've got a handsome trunk carrier, Tabbie," she said, hugging her roommate.

An hour later, Tabbie and Eric waved good-bye to Phoebe.

XXXXX

During lunch in the cafeteria, Tabbie grinned at Eric. "It's time for us to explore our relationship. Junior year is known as a time for harvesting your boy and claiming him as yours—or the reverse, but I'm learning to claim my power. I hope you still like me."

His face brightened; he put up his fists. "I like a strong woman. You'll keep me on my toes."

"Let's go out to a swinging branch I discovered near my old dorm," she said, knowing that she could retain her strength there; she had with Thomas her freshman year.

They walked hand-in-hand till they came to the swinging branch and sat side by side on the curved low limb.

She lifted his hand and kissed it. "Eric, I still love you. I missed our dates last year. I'm glad neither of us found a replacement."

"I've never stopped loving you. You're mine for a lifetime. When can we start dating again?"

"Right away." She smiled. "My birthday is on October 16. Let's wait until then to start our touching dance. I'll be twenty and more marriageable. Whoops, I didn't mean to say that. I do have sexual feelings for you, and we can discuss how far to go." Tabbie was pleased and proud that she could talk openly about an embarrassing topic.

"Let's start kissing now. In October, we'll loosen the brakes and roll into each other." He swooped down, gripped her gently, and kissed her entire face. She lost her balance, and they fell to the ground.

He wrapped his corduroy legs around her jean legs. "Let's go after it now," he said, righting his body.

"Eric," she said, pushing him away. "Other students come here." As she said that, a couple approached the tree.

"Excuse us," the girl said.

"We're leaving now," Tabbie said, standing and pulling Eric up.

Eric walked her back to her dorm; at the entrance, he nuzzled her neck, whispering, "I can't wait until October."

As Tabbie's birthday plans developed, Eric agreed to drive Tabbie and Suzie to Bradberry. The night before they left, Eric decided to take Tabbie to Pierre's Inn, an extravagant French restaurant sixty miles from their college campus. He had eaten there once; his parents had taken him there for his birthday, and the cheapest item on the menu was $30; it was a steak the size of a small hand. He had never returned. Usually he took Tabbie to McDonalds, ten minutes away and cheap; the top price was $10, but Eric remembered Suzie's advice: "Spend money on Tabbie so she knows you love her."

When he picked Tabbie up at her dorm, he saw a *Sound of Music* Maria wearing a white blouse embroidered with green and blue flowers, a cinch belt, and a green puckered skirt. He wanted to grab her and sing *Maria*.

"Go ahead and kiss her," Suzie said. "I know you want to. I see it in your eyes."

He swept Tabbie up, kissed her lips, and they left. At dinner that night, they shared escargots, lamb, and asparagus. They left hungry but happy.

On the drive back to the dorm, Eric stopped on a deserted road. "Let's celebrate your birthday early," he said, turning on the heater and moving close to Tabbie.

Tabbie pushed him away. "Remember, Eric, October 16 is the day we can break restrictions."

"But we'll be at your Aunt Phoebe's tomorrow. That's no place to make out."

"The fields are full of fallen trees, humongous rocks, and hideouts. We'll find a place."

The weekend of October 15 and 16, Eric drove Suzie and Tabbie to Bradberry. Tabbie had already told Suzie that she thought Eric was going to give her an engagement ring. In the car, Tabbie and Suzie teased him about it.

"Let's play twenty questions," Suzie said. "It's about your gift to Tabbie. I'll start. Is it big or little?"

"Big," Eric said.

"Is it round or square?" Tabbie asked.

"Square."

None of Eric's answers pointed to a small round ring.

"Eric," Tabbie said with surprise, "Your nose is getting longer each time you lie, and it's not becoming to you."

He took his right hand off the steering wheel to feel his nose. It wasn't longer. Glancing in the mirror, he swerved to the right. He stepped on the brakes, but it was too late. Two right tires went into a ditch, and the mucky mud kept him from driving the car out.

"Eric, look what you've done," Tabbie said. "We're stuck. If we try to get out, we'll sludge in the mud."

"Do you have rubber boots for us, Eric?" Suzie asked.

"Stay calm and still. There's a red car coming up behind us. Perhaps there's a muscle man inside." He stepped out, holding on to the car to keep from falling into the mud.

The driver stopped. Much to Eric's disappointment, she was a curly, redheaded college student dressed in a red sweater and slacks. "You are in trouble," she said, looking at the car. "Do you have passengers in there?" she asked, glancing through the windows. She gasped. "My god, who are you? That's my sister in there. Her name is Tabbie. I'm going to rescue her."

Dorcas returned to the trunk of her car, grabbed her black galoshes (she kept them there for emergencies), put them on, and walked over to Eric. She didn't like the sloshy noise they made; she felt like a fireman. Today she'd play that role.

"Move away, I have to get these girls out." She stepped, sinking in the mud, and opened the door. Suddenly she realized she needed a man to lift them out. She wasn't strong enough.

As she was thinking what to do next, a man in a pickup stopped, stepped out, and examined Eric's car. He was wearing tall rubber boots.

"I'll trade mine for yours," Dorcas said, pointing at them.

"No way." He stepped sideways, walking over to Eric. "I have a crank. I'll attach it to the right fender and pull slowly."

Dorcas yelled through the window to Tabbie, "Don't be scared! This fellow knows what he's doing. You'll be back on the road in a minute."

She heard grinding tires, splashing mud, and the car was back on the road.

Eric helped Tabbie climb out of the car. "Are you all right? Move your arms and legs, rotate your head. Any pain?"

"I'm fine." Tabbie looked at Dorcas. "What are you doing here? Phoebe told me you were rehearsing a play at college."

"Mom gave me a day off. Who is this?" She pointed at Eric.

"My boyfriend. Eric, meet my twin Dorcas."

They shook hands.

"I've heard about you. You're cuter than she described."

"Maybe she didn't want you to steal me.

You have a reputation of being a queen disregarding rules of civility."

In the silence, they heard Suzie call out, "Hey, I'm in here too."

Eric walked over, reached for her arm, and pulled her out gently.

"Are you all right?" he asked. "Turn your head, reach down, and touch your toes. Good." He turned and motioned to Tabbie. "Let's drive to your dad's."

"I'll take Suzie," Dorcas said, and they disappeared into her car.

XXXXX

On the way to Bradberry, Eric glanced down at Tabbie's hand. "I hope your fingers didn't swell. I've got something for this one." He picked her ring finger up to kiss, and the car swerved again.

"Eric, keep your eyes on the road," Tabbie said, grabbing his arm. "Aunt Phoebe will be ecstatic that Dorcas came. Now you'll get to know Dorcas through your own eyes, not mine. You can form your own opinion. Don't be too impressed by her intelligence and give her my ring."

"If she doesn't treat you with respect, I'll boot her bottom," he said.

"Eric, 'Peace at all costs' is our family motto," she said. "Why did you lie about my ring and say it was big and square?"

"That's the package that I wrapped it in," he said, laughing.

"Next time, be honest. See the trouble it got us in?" She breathed in deeply, closed her eyes, and slept for the next forty miles.

"We're in Bradberry, birthday girl." Eric shook her arm.

"Turn left here and then right on East Hill Road," she said, stretching her arms and rubbing granules out of her eyes.

As Eric gunned the car up the steep hill, Tabbie saw dust in all directions. "Dorcas must have arrived before we did," she said, winding up the window.

When Eric drove to the house, Phoebe, Richard, Cindy, and Suzie poured out of it, blowing horns and shouting "Happy birthday."

"Where's Dorcas?" Tabbie asked.

"She said she had already wished you happy birthday and is in the bathroom putting lipstick on," Phoebe said.

Eric handed Tabbie's hand to Cindy. "Will you walk her in? I want to talk to Mr. Thorndike."

When everyone disappeared inside, Eric spoke to Richard. "Sir, I'd like to marry Tabbie. I want to give her an engagement ring today for her birthday."

Richard looked at him, half-surprised. "Eric, our family likes you and welcomes you into it. My only request is that you both finish college first. You'll need the degree to become a high school principal, and she'll need hers to become a teacher."

"Those are our plans, sir."

"Then she's yours, and you're hers. She's a strong, capable, beautiful woman with plans to work and accomplish the unusual. I won't allow anyone—husband, sister, foe—to tangle her into submission."

"My thoughts and feelings exactly. Thank you, sir."

They shook hands, and Richard went inside.

Eric appeared five minutes later, his hands weighed down with a large box. He looked around. "Can Tabbie open this now?"

Everyone nodded, except for Dorcas. "Remember our ritual, we alternate opening gifts. Where is mine to open?" she asked.

No one handed her one.

"I didn't expect you, Dorcas, and haven't wrapped yours," Phoebe said. "I was going to bring it to you next Saturday when I come to see your play."

She looked at Richard. "Dad, where is yours?"

Cindy said, "Ditto."

Dorcas looked at Tabbie expectantly. "I know my thoughtful sister plans to give me one."

Tabbie shook her head. "Mine is in the dorm. I've already wrapped it in brown paper, put postage stamps on, and it's ready to mail."

"I might as well drive back to college," she said. She turned around, climbed in her car, and left.

Phoebe looked at Eric. "I guess Tabbie has told you about her temper."

Eric nodded. "Sit down, Tabbie, so you can open your present." He pushed the large box to her.

Tabbie smiled. "Who has scissors?"

Cindy went to the kitchen, brought a pair back, and handed them to Tabbie.

"Thanks," she said, cutting the large box. She yanked the cardboard away and found another box.

"Open that," Eric said.

As she ripped it apart, she found a smaller gift wrapped in gold paper. The tag said, "Till death do us part."

Tabbie grinned and handed the box to Eric. As he got down on his knees, the door opened.

Dorcas came in. "I stopped at the bottom of the hill and realized how rude I was to everyone. I'd like to apologize."

"Shhh," Phoebe said, moving her lips.

Eric slipped a small diamond ring on Tabbie's finger. "It was my grandmother's engagement ring."

"Oh, Eric, it's beautiful," she said, leaning over to kiss him.

"Twenty years old and you're engaged, sister. Isn't there a law against that?" Dorcas asked, looking over at Richard.

He shook his head.

"Or a family rule about sex before age twenty-one?" Dorcas looked over at Phoebe.

"When Eric pledges his love with an engagement ring, they're on their own," Cindy said.

"Let's bring the cake and ice cream out," Phoebe said. She and Cindy went into the kitchen. They came out carrying a cake with thick white frosting, cut in two halves, twenty-one candles were on each. Phoebe put her half in front of Dorcas and Cindy put hers in front of Tabbie.

"They're both maple," Phoebe said, "so no grabbing or hitting like five-year-olds."

"Oh, let them, Aunt Phoebe," Eric said. "I'd like to see who wins."

CHAPTER 8

In early May, forsythia as yellow as farm eggs bloomed across Tabbie's college campus. Perky little crocuses were popping up everywhere and getting trampled by students. Tabbie and Suzie wanted to dress in yellow shirts and patrol them by putting up signs Don't Step on Me, but there were too few students who cared. Tabbie felt sad when she came across crushed ones.

Tabbie, Eric, and Suzie helped each other study for exams; they passed their courses and looked forward to getting their diplomas on graduation day.

Tabbie's and Dorcas's celebrations were on the same day, the last week in May. Eric, Cindy, and Richard attended Tabbie's graduation; Phoebe and Bess went to Dorcas's. Tabbie's heart melted. She wanted Phoebe, the most important woman in her world, to attend hers. She consoled herself that the following week Phoebe would be the matron of honor at her wedding. She had asked Suzie to be her maid of honor, which had infuriated Dorcas.

"That goes to the sister of the bride," Dorcas had said. "Don't you love and respect me?"

"Yes, but I make my own decisions for my wedding," Tabbie had replied. "You've planned your future of acting in New York City, and I haven't interfered." Tabbie was glad that Dorcas's life was going to be separate from hers. She would no longer be Dorcas's handmaiden. She was becoming a married woman who would make joint decisions with her husband. They would honor each other.

Eric and Tabbie met with Pastor Tate of the Congregational Church several weeks before the wedding. He was dressed in a gray suit and a matching gray tie when he sat down with Eric and Tabbie in his office to advise them on their conjugal roles. "In Ephesians, it advises that the wife should be subjugated to her husband," he said in a low, dignified voice. "Are you in agreement with that?" he asked, staring down at them over his glasses.

"We are going to be equal in our marriage," Eric said.

"I take Ephesians very seriously," Pastor Tate said, shaking his head. "This has happened to me before with college-educated couples. I'll ask Pastor Todd from Grafton to perform the ceremony. He feels fine leaving that part of Ephesians out of the service."

"Thank you, sir," Eric said. "Will he have a key to the church?"

"Yes, he is marrying more couples like you." Pastor Tate got up from his chair, straightened his jacket, and turned out the light. "I wish you God's grace." He shook their hands, waiting for them to leave.

"Thank you, Pastor Tate," Tabbie said, standing up. "We'd like you to come to our wedding and to the reception afterwards."

"I'm sorry, but I won't be able to. I only go to weddings that I perform," the minister said. He coughed slightly. "Please apologize to your aunt Phoebe for me."

"Would you like to come to our rehearsal dinner, sir?" Eric asked. "My brother, who is a bouncer at a bar in Boston, and his wife, who dances for tips, will be there."

The minister cleared his throat and declined. "Please ask Miss Phoebe to bring the check to church this Sunday, put it in the plate, and mark it 'Thorndike and Stutsman wedding.'"

After Tabbie and Eric left the church, Tabbie nudged Eric's arm. "Why did you tell him that about your brother?" she asked, laughing.

"He was irritating me with all his lowly women stuff, so I thought a joke would be fun."

"I love you, Eric," she said, hugging him. "I won't have a chance to get depressed or anxious, married to you. You'll keep me giggling."

That night, when Tabbie lay down in bed to fall asleep, she prayed, "Thank you, Lord, for Eric's and my love. I am marrying the kindest man in the world."

XXXXX

June came quickly. Both girls graduated; the wedding was the following weekend. At ten o'clock on Friday morning, Phoebe and Tabbie were gluing daisies on the final place cards for the rehearsal dinner that evening. As Phoebe played a scratched record of Wagner's wedding march on her old victrola, Dorcas and Kate marched in.

"Did we miss the wedding?" Dorcas asked. She was already dressed for the dinner, looking elegant in her red suede skirt and red scoop-necked silk top.

Kate had dressed in a red dress with feathers stitched on. She smelled of Chanel No. 5. They sat on the sofa opposite the table. "Ronald is so sorry he can't come, but he wants you to have this," Kate said, handing Tabbie a bottle of Chanel No. 5.

"How wonderful!" Tabbie said, her voice rising melodically. "Phoebe, I'll squirt you."

"Where are we having the dinner?" Dorcas asked.

"At the Curved River Motel on Route 30 across from the Gap Horse Farm," Tabbie said, smiling.

"You can't have it there, Tabbie," Dorcas said. "The smell of the horse pies will make your guests sick."

"No one will be able to taste the hors d'oeuvres that we ordered from the Stoddard Inn," Kate said. "Why did you decide to have it there?"

"It costs too much money at the Inn, and Phoebe is paying for it. Dad and Cindy are paying for our wedding night. You haven't offered to pay for anything." Tabbie looked straight at her mother, demanding a response.

"Ronald and I will pay for a play for you to see in New York City. You can stay in our apartment at Gramercy Park."

"Where are you going for your honeymoon?" Dorcas asked.

"That's a secret between Eric and me."

""I bet Phoebe knows," Kate said, glaring at Phoebe. She had been envious of Tabbie's closeness to Phoebe since she was a child. "Does your dad know?"

"Only Eric and I know," Tabbie repeated.

"Let's switch to another topic, Mother," Dorcas reproached her. She turned to Tabbie. "Can we see your dress for tonight? I promise we won't pass judgment."

"I don't have time to put it on, but you can see it on the hanger." Tabbie went to her old room and came out with a green linen dress with a straight top and flowers embroidered on it. The skirt was straight and reached midlength.

"It's pretty, sister, but not elegant. I wish you would have let me pick one out for you in New York City," Dorcas said.

"Cindy helped me pick it out. We both love it," Tabbie said.

"No wonder it's plain," Kate said. "Cindy seems clueless about fashion."

XXXXX

On Friday night, thunder, lightning, and heavy rain poured down on the motel picnic area. Tabbie called the staff and asked if they could move the rehearsal dinner to the dining room.

"Of course we can," the main waitress said.

Within an hour, the motel staff had decorated the dining room with vases of black-eyed susans, daisies, and ferns. They had twisted strings of ivy across linen tablecloths.

The rehearsal dinner began at six o'clock.

Dressed in a brown corduroy jacket with a daisy in his buttonhole, Eric held Tabbie's hand at the head table. She looked beautiful in her green dress and a band of daisies in her long brown hair.

Bess, who was sitting beside Richard, wore a purple flowered skirt, a lavender blouse, and a necklace with a round plastic picture of a cat. She looked over at the main table where Dorcas and Kate were sitting. "Dorcas looks lovely tonight," she commented. "If she weren't so passionate about acting, she could be a high-end model in Hollywood, wearing everything from bikinis to gowns, but then we'd never see her."

"Dad looks handsome in his suit," Dorcas whispered. "He's a good dad. Why did you leave him, Kate?"

"He was boring and didn't understand my love for acting. I wanted someone passionate about it, like Ronald."

"You and I are two of a kind," Dorcas said.

After the meal, waiters filled champagne glasses, and the toasts began.

Eric stood and clinked Tabbie's glass. "Tomorrow begins the most fabulous day of my life. I'm marrying a gifted, sweet, beautiful woman. I don't know how an ordinary student like me could win her heart, but I did." He raised his glass. "To Tabbie, my bride."

Everyone echoed, "A toast to Tabbie."

When Eric sat, Tabbie whispered in his ear, "I wish you hadn't said *sweet* and *beautiful*. That's been my tag since childhood. I'm new, Eric. Haven't you seen my harsh side?"

"You don't have one," he said, kissing her.

Richard stood up next. "I am the lucky father of twins." He looked at Dorcas and held up his glass. "Dorcas, who is married to her acting career, and my loving daughter, Tabbie, who has true beauty in her face and heart. Since childhood, she has rescued hurt birds, put bandages on her aunt Phoebe when she cut her fingers in the kitchen and one on me when thistles scratched my arms and legs. Eric, you are marrying the woman of most men's dreams. May you both be happy."

Everyone stood, raised their glasses, and chanted, "To our beautiful bride, Tabbie."

Eric's father stood and praised Eric next. "Tabbie, you are marrying a loyal, hardworking, kind son, whose humor will keep you laughing."

Phoebe stood. "I have been lucky enough to raise these two girls, Dorcas and Tabbie. Each has a different part of my heart. Dorcas's quick mind has kept me on my toes since she was small. Tabbie has the loving spirit of an angel whose wings touch people who struggle.

She'll be a wonderful teacher, wife, and mother. Let's toast our lovely bride, Tabbie."

"We love you Tabbie," the guests called out. "We love you, Eric." They toasted him.

Phoebe's toast was the last one, and everyone got up to leave.

XXXXX

The sun shone brightly on Saturday, Tabbie's wedding day. Guests gathered in front of the church, chatting, until they heard the old bells ring at twelve o'clock. They whispered and hurried into the church to find seats. Richard had invited a few of his teacher friends, some who had taught Tabbie. Phoebe had asked a couple of her elementary school teachers who had worked with Tabbie when she was younger. Tabbie and Eric had asked a few of their college friends to attend. Some local people were sitting in the pews: Dr. Otley, who had treated Tabbie for mumps, measles, and an emergency appendicitis; Miss Sarah, the local librarian; and Dr. Harper, Tabbie's dentist and Thomas's father.

As the organist played the wedding march, the bridesmaids came down the aisle. Tabbie had planned that Suzie and Dorcas wear soft blue cotton dresses, but Dorcas had complained that blue was not her color and had swapped it out for a bright red one without telling her sister. Phoebe wore a teal green dress, and they all carried bouquets of field flowers. Eric's brother and his roommate from college escorted them.

Eric was dressed in a light brown suit; he and his father climbed up the stairs to the altar. The organist changed the tune to "Here Comes the Bride," and Tabbie, looking beautiful in a white percale dress embroidered with flowers around the neck, came down the aisle on Richard's arm.

When Tabbie reached the altar, she looked straight at Eric, who smiled at her. She smiled back. She was nervous and didn't want to look out into the church now. She promised herself she would, when she returned down the aisle as Eric's wife.

As Eric turned toward the guests, he greeted them with a grin.

The pastor started the service, and everyone listened to the familiar words, which brought tears and memories to many people. When the pastor asked, "Who gives this woman to this man?" Richard said, "I do," and stepped down to sit next to Cindy. Kate stood up and said, "I do," before sitting back down next to Bess.

The pastor continued, "Does anyone here have a reason why these two should not become husband and wife?"

Silence in the church.

"Then I pronounce Tabbie and Eric husband and wife. Eric, you may kiss your bride."

As Tabbie and Eric walked down the aisle, Tabbie glowed like the gold at the end of a blessed rainbow.

Eric drove Tabbie up East Hill Road to Phoebe's house; the reception was in the backyard. "Tabbie, do you want to detour down the creek road and make out?" he teased.

"We're married now and don't have to hide behind trees," she said, poking him. "Hurry or we'll be late for our own party."

When they arrived, they saw cars were pulling into the driveway. They found a spot reserved for them and walked behind the house. The sound and soul of happiness filled the backyard, a mowed field; friends' voices chattered like chickadees and cardinals.

Eric and Tabbie stood at the refreshment table to greet guests and thank them for coming.

Richard poured champagne into plastic cups, Cindy served pimiento cheese and cucumber sandwiches decrusted and cut in triangles, and Suzie served orange sherbet and ginger ale punch at the far end of the table.

Thirty minutes later, Dorcas announced the arrival of the three-tier dark chocolate wedding cake. ""A taste of New York City," she said. "Come and get your serving before it disappears."

Eric fed Tabbie a piece of sticky, sweet frosting-cake, and she stuffed some into his mouth. Napkins had already been handed out, so they licked each other's fingers and mouths like kindergarteners.

The guests clapped. "To our bride and groom."

Each looked at each other and nodded.

"Time for us to go," Tabbie whispered. She collected Suzie, and they went inside. Twenty minutes later, Tabbie came out in her green linen suit and walked to the side porch.

Cindy announced loudly, "Single women, gather. The bride is throwing her bouquet."

A gaggle of geese, all ages, stood beneath the porch. The bundle of daisies floated down, and Bess caught it. Voices yelled, "Throw it again. Bess doesn't need a husband. It's Dorcas's turn."

Dorcas said loudly, "My plans don't include a husband. If they did, I'd want him to be an actor."

Phoebe took the bouquet from Bess. "I'll put it in water until you come back, Tabbie. It can decorate your kitchen table."

When people saw the bouquet in Phoebe's hands, they cheered, "Hurray, Phoebe is next." She shook her head and joined the others in throwing petals and pink confetti at Tabbie, who was running toward the truck.

Eric had washed and waxed his red pickup. He was surprised to see "Just Married," written with red lipstick on the side window.

Tabbie and Eric waved to the guests, honked their horn, and drove down the hill. He stopped at the garage in town to wash the lipstick off. He felt better driving to the Stoddard Inn as an ordinary couple. Otherwise, locals would chase them, throwing tubes of Vaseline and washcloths, yelling, "You'll need these tonight." It was a summer game for the kids in high school.

As he turned the curves on Route 30, he looked over at Tabbie. "You know who annoys me? Dorcas. When we find a place to live, can she visit just once a year?"

They arrived at the Stoddard Inn and went inside, its beauty overwhelmed them. The floral wallpaper and white molding provided the background for elegant maple tables with china lamps. A couch was covered with cream-colored tapestry with horses and carriages woven in it.

Tabbie sat down while Eric registered them for the night. He had just taken Tabbie's hand to lead her upstairs when the outside door opened. Kate and Dorcas walked in.

"What the hell are you doing here? Why can't you leave us alone?" he said angrily.

Kate said, "I know the owner of this inn, and he said that he will serve you and Tabbie the gourmet trout meal at no cost."

"That's fine, but if you two are planning to stay here tonight, we won't." Eric went up to the desk and told the young man, "Please cancel our reservation."

"If that's what you want to do, sir, but you'll have to pay half of the bill since you are telling me so late."

Eric yanked his wallet out of his pocket and pulled out a $100 bill. "There," he said, glancing angrily at Kate and Dorcas. "You've spoiled our wedding night. If you ever get married, beware of my fiery interference."

Dorcas caught a quick glimpse of how she was spoiling their special night. She stared at Tabbie, who was wiping away tears with Eric's linen handkerchief. Dorcas couldn't relate to the passion of a wedding night, but she had been trying to feel Juliet's longing for Romeo. She felt a pang and whispered to her mother, "I think we should stay somewhere else and let them have this night to themselves."

"Don't be ridiculous, Dorcas. We've reserved our room, and so have Eric and Tabbie."

"Mom, I'm canceling ours," Dorcas said, telling the man at the desk that she and Miss Kate were leaving.

"It's too late," Eric said, picking up the suitcases. He took Tabbie's arm, and they walked out of the inn and to the truck.

"We'll leave if you want to stay," Dorcas yelled, but Kate shouted, "Happy honeymoon! We love you!" and waved good-bye.

"What bitches!" Eric said as he drove off.

"Where shall we stay? In the truck?" Tabbie asked.

"I know of a place in Glennsboro." He leaned over and kissed her.

He drove south for fifteen minutes and parked on Lucky Street in front of a tall old building made of brick, with the eaves painted red. It looked like an old lady sitting high, scrutinizing the town. In the early 1900s, it had been an elegant hotel, but today, its face was peeling, bricks were missing, and a railroad passed behind it.

"Here we are," Eric said. "Here's our Cinderella Castle." He laughed. "Our first adventure as a married couple. We'll plan a lot of adventures since we won't be teaching this summer."

"School principals work year round," she reminded him.

"But while I'm getting my masters, we'll have time off." He grinned.

"I guess our baby can travel with us," Tabbie said.

"What baby?" he asked, startled.

"Perhaps we'll create one tonight."

CHAPTER 9

The first year of Eric's graduate program in administration, he and Tabbie rented a small apartment off the University of Vermont campus. His grades were excellent, and he would do an internship next year in a junior high school. Tabbie co-taught deaf and blind children and those with cerebral palsy in the university's special-needs preschool program. She was learning to sign while her partner- teacher mastered braille. Eric and Tabbie's happiness released energy, and they made love nightly.

The first day in August, Tabbie missed her period. "Eric, I think we're pregnant," she told him two weeks later. "I'm feeling nauseated, as if I were on a fishing boat in the ocean." She swayed, looked pale, and ran to the bathroom.

He followed her.

She was on the cold tile floor, leaning against the porcelain toilet bowl, vomiting. He handed her a dry blue towel to clean up and pressed a wet one on her forehead.

"I think I can stand now," she said, lifting her arms so he could pull her up.

Eric walked her into their small bedroom, where she lay down on their bed. When she felt better, he tapped her tummy, put his ears to her belly, and listened for a sound. "Son, are you comfortable in there?"

Tabbie sat up and bopped his head with her hand. "We don't know if it's a boy or girl. You told me that you wanted a daughter first so you can hug and kiss her. You said you might feel funny kissing a boy."

"You're right." He tilted her head and stared into her eyes. "You don't have Dorcas's genes in there, do you?"

"If I do, we'll cuddle him or her into a loveable, kind child. Maybe our baby will have Dorcas's brain and my kindness."

He banged her head softly. "You know you're smart. He'll have some of my genes too: personality, brilliance, and super handsomeness." Eric bowed with a flourish.

They laughed. "Can we still make love when I'm pregnant?" Tabbie asked.

"I think so. Let's make an appointment with the doctor, and we'll write a list of questions. I'll ask some of my friends who delivered their babies. You do the same."

A few days later, Tabbie had gathered three names, telephone numbers, and descriptions: Dr. L., kind, takes time to answer questions; Dr. R., didactic, puts you to sleep, his way or no way; and Dr. S., flexible, will consider natural childbirth with midwife.

The next Saturday, when she and Eric were eating breakfast, she read the list to him.

"Who do you want, Tabbie? You're the one birthing the baby."

"I've already set up an appointment with Dr. Lansing next Tuesday, when you're not in class. I'd like you to come with me, Eric."

"Of course I'll come," he said, grinning.

The following Tuesday, Tabbie wore a bright blue maternity dress that she had bought. "Do you like it?" she asked, as they left their apartment.

"Yes, but I like what's in it better." He kissed her. "I think it's a little early to be wearing that. You're going to bias the doctor before he examines you. Do you have your list of questions?"

"Yes." She opened her purse and held them up.

When they got to Dr. L.'s office at the edge of the medical school campus, she filled out six sheets of paper, giving her medical history. "I hope the antidepressants I took in high school won't hurt our baby," she whispered to Eric.

"Add that to your questions," Eric said.

Soon Dr. Lansing came in, introduced himself, and asked them to follow him to his office. He glanced down at her sheet of paper. "You probably want to ask some things, but I'm going to examine you first, Mrs. Stutsman, to make sure you're pregnant."

He went out to the hallway and called his nurse. She took Tabbie into the examining room, where he joined them. He had a small mirror, which he inserted into her. "I see your uterus lining is thickening, and there's a little shape attached to it. Congratulations, Miss Tabbie. Shall we go tell your husband?"

XXXXX

When Tabbie and Eric got home, she ran through the house, yelling, "We're pregnant!" She bumped into Eric. "Hug me and the baby." He did, but then became serious.

"We've got to set money aside to pay for this," he said.

"Let's celebrate before we worry," Tabbie said, pushing him into the living room chair. "Who do you think I should call first, Phoebe or Dad?" Richard and Cindy were no longer living with Phoebe; they had bought a small house in town closer to their schools.

"Your choice. I'll take care of my parents," Eric said.

"You're not much help. Let's invite Phoebe, Dad, and Cindy for lunch this Saturday. I'll tell Kate and Dorcas later."

XXXXX

On Saturday, Tabbie made cheese fondue. She cut tiger lilies and daisies at the side of the road and put them in a blue vase on the table. She placed a silver rattle that she had had as a baby beside the flowers. As she dusted the house, she sang, "She'll be coming around the mountain when she comes." When she finished, she sang, "He'll be coming around the mountain when he comes."

Richard drove Cindy and Phoebe from Bradberry. They had made reservations for the night at the Holiday Inn, but they drove to Eric and Tabbie's apartment first. They had seen it once when they had moved Tabbie and Eric's furniture in. It looked cozier now. The front door opened into the living room, where they had a comfy couch and several wooden chairs with cushions. Eric's desk was in the corner. The kitchen was located beside the living room. The sink, refrigerator, and stove filled the small space. Off the kitchen was a sunroom, where Tabbie and Eric had put a dining room table. Their bedroom opened off the sunroom.

Richard carried in a large ice chest and put it on the linoleum floor in the kitchen. After everyone hugged, Phoebe took out an apple pie and put it on the counter. Cindy removed a cellophane bag of lettuce, tomatoes, celery, carrots, and olives for a salad. Phoebe took out sugary cinnamon muffins from Madge's bakery for tomorrow's breakfast.

"You brought too much," Tabbie said, kissing her cheek.

"You're making the entree, you amazing woman," Phoebe said, never tiring of praising Tabbie.

"Hold your compliments until we eat," Eric said. "This is the first time she has cooked fondue."

"I hope you're hungry. It's ready," Tabbie said. "Phoebe, will you put the plates on the table, please?"

Phoebe took a stack of five plates into the next room. "Tabbie, you're pregnant," Phoebe screamed. She shook the rattle and squeezed Tabbie gently. "Richard, Cindy, she's pregnant. Go hug her."

Richard leaned forward to kiss Tabbie, leaving a space the size of a baby between them.

Cindy ran her fingers through Tabbie's hair. "Will you let me give her milk and oatmeal?" Cindy didn't plan to have children of her own. Richard had told her he had already raised two children and she was raising twenty in her classroom.

"Of course, Cindy. When neither of us is teaching in the summer, we can take turns driving back and forth between Bradberry and here."

Richard slapped Eric on the shoulder. "There's a chance you may have twins. Are you ready for that?"

"If you stick around to help with the diapers." Eric poured wine. "A toast to the babies." He and Richard touched glasses.

Tabbie, Phoebe, and Cindy were buzzing about maternity clothes, hospitals, and baby furniture. Tabbie turned around when she heard the toast. "Eric, Dr. Lansing says that we're having one baby, not two. How much wine have you guys downed?"

"A glass. At least we haven't talked triplets, honey."

They laughed themselves through supper. They stabbed chunks of bread with their long-handled forks and dipped them in the pot of bubbling cheese fondue. When they brought the forks back to their mouths, the cheese stretched like gum. Tabbie brought two pairs of scissors to the table to cut resistant strands.

After swallowing his forkful, Richard looked over at Eric. "Encourage Tabbie to nurse so she takes night duty. Kate started ours on a bottle from the start. I was the night feeder." He yawned, remembering it. "Do you think you missed bonding with your mother?" he asked Tabbie.

"Her nipples would have cut Dorcas and me like knife points. I bonded with you and Aunt Phoebe." She squeezed their hands. "Thank you for all your love. Will you give it to our baby too?"

Two voices sang out, "Absolutely."

"Have you told your mother and Dorcas yet?" Phoebe asked.

Tabbie shook her head.

"Once you do, they'll plot a career in acting for the little guy or gal," Richard said, shaking his head.

XXXXX

Several weeks after Tabbie discovered her pregnancy, she called Dorcas. "Dorcas, I'm going to have a baby. It's due in April. You're going to be an aunt."

"I'm going to be a mother first," Dorcas replied. "I'm two months pregnant."

"You're not married," Tabbie said with surprise. "Who's the father?"

"A producer I've been sleeping with."

"Have you told Kate or Dad?"

"Mom wants me to have an abortion. She knows of a clinic that does them."

"Don't do that, Dorcas. I'll try to find a Bradberry couple that wants a child but can't get pregnant. Have you asked Dad and Cindy?"

"No, I think they're a little old. That would be something like incest, a dad raising his daughter's child. I could write a Shakespearean play on that! Are you starting to show yet?"

"No, I think that begins the end of the third month. Do you remember when we were small? We used to stuff pillows under our shirts. When we pulled the pillows out, there were two baby dolls in a small crib. After ten minutes of nursing them with our tiny nipples and changing their diapers, you went off to make up plays with your stuffed animals. I spent the rest of the day taking care of them."

"Tabbie, you don't need to point out that I'd make a lousy mother. I know that. I'll either have an abortion or give birth and adopt the child out," Dorcas said.

"Don't abort yet. Give me a week to check around for prospective parents."

"I may go ahead anyway. No one wants a pregnant actress!"

"Isn't there some play where the main character becomes pregnant and carries a child? You could play that part."

"Maybe in the Christmas story, but I'd have to do that in a church, and I don't believe in the miracle birth. I have to go, Tabbie. I'm about to throw up."

"Don't do anything for a week, Dorcas," Tabbie pleaded as she heard the phone click.

At the kitchen table, Tabbie pondered who could raise a child. *Dad and Cindy? Cindy would make a great mom.* Tabbie pulled a pad of paper toward her and wrote their names on it. *What about Bess?* she thought. *No, Bess would raise a baby like a kitten and give it milk in a saucer and teach him or her to poop in the litter box!* Bess's name didn't go on the list.

"I could raise two babies," she said with surprise. She hadn't thought of herself as the mother of Dorcas's child. She wrote *Tabbie* on her list. "What about Phoebe? She raised both of us." *No, she's tired and has two years until retirement and freedom.*

Tabbie was expanding her list, making pros and cons for each name on it, when Eric came home from an evening class.

He kissed her. "You look so serious about your grocery list, Tabbie."

"It's a different kind of list, Eric. Dorcas called to say she's two months pregnant."

"What? That bitch doesn't even have a boyfriend. Is it an immaculate conception?"

"Eric, don't talk like that. Our baby will hear. He or she will come out tense and cursing."

"Sorry, but how did she become pregnant? Who is the father?"

"Some producer she's been working with. Can we raise her baby, Eric?"

"Certainly not," Eric snapped. Whenever they talked about Dorcas, he became impatient. "We don't have the money to raise two babies, and I certainly don't want one with Dorcas's genes. Dorcas is a thief. She stole your personality."

"Eric, I don't think we can let her abort."

"What about adoption into another family? Couples pray daily to get pregnant, and it never happens. I know someone in the education department whose wife just had her third miscarriage."

"Oh, Eric, will you tell them?"

"Sure, but I won't mention that Dorcas is a selfish, self-centered redhead who has to have her way. I'll let them think she is like you."

Later that night, Tabbie called Cindy and Richard. "Cindy I've got something exciting to tell you and Dad. Will you ask him to get on the other phone?"

When he picked up the phone, Richard spoke first. "Tabbie, how is the baby growing? Does he look like me?"

"Dad, Cindy, Dorcas called to say she's pregnant. She's going to have an abortion if she can't find a couple she approves of to raise him or her." Tabbie stopped and prayed.

Silence. Cindy and Richard were in different rooms. "It's impossible," Richard said in answer to Tabbie's unspoken question. "I'm finished with parenting. I certainly don't feel obligated to Dorcas. She got herself in this trouble, and she can get herself out."

"Richard, don't say no so quickly," Cindy said. "I've told you several times that I'd love to raise a baby. I can't get pregnant, so this is our opportunity."

"Cindy, I've got all I can handle teaching Advanced Literature and mentoring five students. I want to save time and energy for you."

"It's your chance to have a boy, a namesake, who can keep the Thorndike name going," Cindy argued.

"Cindy, you're in a daze. It wouldn't make sense. You'd stop teaching, and we need your income." Cindy and Richard were arguing on the phone as if Tabbie weren't there.

"Tabbie, I'll call you tomorrow with our decision," Cindy said.

XXXXX

At 7:00 a.m. the next day, Cindy called. "Tabbie, Richard has agreed to it. I had to tell him that I would keep working and let Granny Polk down the road keep our baby during the day. She used to rock him when he was small. You and I will be like Elizabeth and Mary in the Bible."

"I'm a beginner, Cindy. I'm reading books on child rearing. Dr. Spock is the expert. You may want to order your own copy. It seems like a day-to-day necessity."

"I've got a lot of things to order. Can I come this weekend and we can shop together? Who do you think should call Dorcas to tell her, you or me? Richard refuses to. He's angry at her."

"I will," Tabbie answered. "I'll call her after school today."

"I hope Dorcas has been eating healthy so the baby is developing well. I don't want it to develop problems. Dorcas doesn't drink, does she?"

"Not very much."

The following afternoon, Tabbie called her sister. "It's Tabbie, Dorcas. I've found a couple who is eager to raise your child, Dad and Cindy."

Silence. "Tabbie, I've talked to Mom. She and I think it's a good idea to have an abortion. I'll miss too many acting opportunities if I'm unavailable for six months."

"Dorcas, you can't kill a child. It's selfish. A child has the right to live. You can visit Dad and Cindy and teach them how to raise your child."

"Tabbie, I've made up my mind. Mom has located a doctor in New York City who can do it. I'm sorry, sister. I've always done what I want, and this time is no different."

"Dorcas, please reconsider. Dad and Cindy would make wonderful parents. They could pay you something for your gift to them."

"Yesterday, I tried out for the part of Lady Macbeth in a theater near Greenwich Village. I got the part! All kinds of theater people will see it, scouting for future talent. I can't turn this down. You may have a famous sister. Your son or daughter will have a celebrity aunt."

"And you may lose a dad and stepmom, Dorcas. They have been so excited, talking about the baby's name, planning to look for a new home. You are ending that with your decision. Why don't you have a miscarriage, Dorcas? It will be easier for all of us."

"I've tried, Tabbie. I've smoked, drank whisky and vodka, pounded my stomach with fists, but the baby is rooted in there."

"Have you thought that this child might have the genes of an actress?"

"I've already made up my mind, sister. Good night."

Tabbie dreaded calling Cindy and her Dad. *How do you break someone's heart?* Thoughts flashed across her mind. *If I give birth to twins, I'll give one to Cindy. I can get pregnant after I deliver this baby and give it to them.* She shook her head. None of these ideas made any sense.

She lifted the receiver and dialed the number. Cindy answered.

"Cindy..." Tabbie's voice sounded tired.

"Tabbie, are you all right? Did you lose the baby? You can help me raise mine."

"Cindy, I'm fine. You lost yours. Dorcas is having an abortion tomorrow."

"She can't. She can't abort a baby that has a loving couple waiting to raise him or her. It's unfair." Cindy was crying. "Who can talk sense into her? Can Kate?"

"She is coaching her to have the abortion."

"Can you?"

"I've tried. She said when the baby gets larger and she shows it will ruin her chances to act."

"Tell her that I'll write a play where the main character is pregnant. I used to write plays and stories when I was in grammar school. I won a ribbon one time."

Silence.

"I've already bought diapers and a changing table," Cindy said sadly.

"I could use them," Tabbie said cautiously

XXXXX

After she hung up, Cindy called Richard who was working late at the high school and told him. "How could you raise such a coldhearted, selfish girl?"

"Cindy, don't blame me," he said with irritation. "Phoebe, Tabbie, and I have worked for years to soften her will and determination. It's all about her. Do I need to come home and hold you?"

"No, I'll call Tabbie again. Maybe we can work out a strategy that will change Dorcas's mind."

"Don't count on it. When Dorcas sets her mind on a path, she doesn't swerve," Richard cautioned.

"I think I need you, Richard. Can you leave school early?"

"I'll be there in ten minutes."

XXXXX

After Eric arrived home, Tabbie came to him.

"We need to think of a way to make Cindy feel better," she said. "Maybe we can ask them to be godparents of our baby and give them all kinds of overnight privileges. I could ask her to be in the delivery room when I give birth," she added with hesitation. "The doctor told me that one person could be present." She went over to Eric and hugged him. "But I want that to be you."

"Thank you for choosing me," he said, hugging her again.

She pushed back and looked up at him with renewed determination. "Eric, I'm going to call Dorcas one more time."

When she reached Dorcas, she sounded sick and exhausted. Instead of her usual perky greeting, she droned, "Hello, Dorcas speaking."

"Dorcas, it's Tabbie. You sound awful."

"I got an infection from the abortion. I've been in bed for a week. Mother is acting my part in *Macbeth*. The kooky doctor forgot to give me antibiotics. What an ordeal! A medical student did it. I'm not bribing any more producers with sex. Did Cindy and Dad get over it?"

"No. But they're going to be godparents of my baby and have all kinds of overnight privileges."

"What does Aunt Phoebe think of me?"

"She's forgiven you."

"Can I talk with her?" Dorcas asked.

"She's busy. I'm sorry you're not feeling well. Take care of yourself. Good-bye." Tabbie hung up.

"Eric, do you think you will ever accept Dorcas as your sister-in-law?"

"Maybe in the future. Let me ask you a question. Do you think you will ever disown her?"

"No. Let's give her a chance to feel remorse, to catch a terrible disease and beg for family love."

CHAPTER 10

Tabbie's pregnancy grew through summer, fall, and winter. Her energy and excitement allowed her to continue teaching in the college preschool program for handicapped children. She woke up at seven in the morning, pulled on her maternity clothes—jeans with an expanding elastic waistband and a floral tent-shaped top—and practiced signing until eight in the morning, when she drove to her classroom. Eric had already left for his job of tutoring confused and failing students at 6:30 a.m.

Tabbie continued to teach her four deaf children, and her coteacher, Sarah, taught braille and mobility to the blind identical twins so they would avoid bumping into tables and chairs. They took turns working with the brother and sister with cerebral palsy, who raced around the room in small wheelchairs.

Tabbie's students slowly learned American Sign Language to replace their own signs: a shove to get the other's attention, a hand to the crotch to say bathroom. Tabbie loved to watch their progress. Sarah worked patiently with her twin girls who had blond curly hair and whose fingers, hands, and ears "saw" instead of their eyes.

As Tabbie's baby grew inside of her, she would come home in the afternoon, sit with her feet propped up on her favorite stool with a picture of a teacher in front of a schoolhouse that Phoebe had crocheted. Christmas was a month away, so she practiced signing: baby Jesus, manger, camels and sheep, and Santa, sleigh, reindeer, and presents.

In the classroom, she held up pictures of Santa, and the two deaf boys shoved the girls out of the way so they could see and touch them. Sarah played Christmas carols for her blind children, but Tabbie's couldn't hear the jingles of bells or the melodies.

At night, when Eric and Tabbie were together, they shared Crock-Pot suppers and talked to their baby. Eric thought it was foolish to talk through a thick layer of skin and uterus to a forming child, but since Tabbie was the early childhood educator, he tried. "We're glad you're ours. We love you already," he said, leaning over Tabbie's stomach and talking. After a couple of minutes, he straightened up and took Tabbie in his arms. "I'd rather create love messages to you," he said, kissing her.

"You can do both," she said, leaning over her stomach and singing "Lullaby and Good Night." "You're a good daddy already."

At night, as they fell asleep, they talked about who might be growing inside of her.

"I see a kicking, squirming, energetic, boy," he said.

"I imagine giving birth to a girl with a round soft-skin face and strands of light brown hair." She imagined her eight-pound baby in her arms, sucking milk out of her full breasts; these were pictures of deep delight.

Tabbie could also easily move to another scene of her holding a baby boy, pulling him close to her and his rooting lips searching her nipples. She folded him into her to protect him, knowing that soon enough her job would be to let him grow independent of her. As sleep settled in, she was holding her baby boy in one arm and her baby girl in another with a heart large enough to love both.

XXXXX

Richard and Cindy talked a lot about their first grandchild. "Initially, I'm going to teach him to roll a large inflatable ball," Richard said.

"As he gets older, it will get smaller and harder like a tennis ball and, finally, a baseball."

"You can play ball with a granddaughter also." Cindy poked him with a knitting needle. She was completing her last row of pink and blue stitches on the blanket she was going to give to Tabbie the upcoming weekend.

When they arrived on Saturday morning, Cindy handed it to Eric. He pulled it out of the tissue paper and shook it to see the size.

"Is it big enough for twin boys? One will be sweet like Tabbie and the other hardworking like me. We'll toss them up in the air and then catch them. Boys like that kind of thing."

"Girls do too," Tabbie said, refusing to believe that there was an actual difference between the sexes. "Culture makes us believe that girls are sissies. Mine might be a tomboy. If it's a girl, I'll let her tumble and roughhouse with you, Eric. If it's a boy, he can color with me."

XXXXX

In mid-March, at 6:00 a.m., Tabbie felt birth pains. She had prayed aloud each night, "God, please let me have a healthy baby. I could raise a deaf, blind, or retarded child, but I'd prefer a normal one." Guilt over saying this hit her with a contraction, and her mind and body hurt. "Sorry, Lord. I'll love whomever you give me."

As the contractions continued, she turned on the light. She timed the pain—every five minutes. She shook Eric. "I think our baby is coming. Let's go to the hospital."

They dressed quickly. For a week, she had put her gray wool jumper and floral blouse on a bedroom chair. She hurriedly slipped them on. Eric pulled out jeans, a crew-neck sweater, and sneakers from the closet.

XXXXX

When they arrived at the hospital, a nurse helped Tabbie climb on a stretcher and rolled her down the hall. The loudspeakers were calling doctors to operating and emergency rooms. "Dr. Adams, report to room A quickly. Dr. Gourley, they need you in the emergency room now!"

Tabbie's nurse pushed her to room C and asked her, "Who is your doctor?"

"Dr. Lansing," Eric answered. "Tell him to come quickly. I don't know how to deliver babies."

"Dr. Wright is covering for Dr. Lansing tonight. I'll wake him right away. He is sleeping on a cot in his office. Remember to breathe in deeply, dear. It will help with the pain. I'll go get the doctor. He'll check you to see how many centimeters you're dilated. By the frequency of your contractions, I'd guess around eight. Mr. Stutsman, Dr. Wright is going to ask you to leave the room as soon as he arrives. It's regulations. As soon as the baby is born, I'll come get you. I'm going to fetch Dr. Wright." The nurse left the room.

"Eric, I wanted you to be in here to see our baby come." Tabbie whimpered.

"I'll push through the door the minute the nurse announces his or her arrival. I love you," he said, leaning over and kissing her on her lips. "You're brave and will be fine." He blew kisses from the doorway.

Tabbie was alone for ten minutes before the doctor arrived. She couldn't think beyond the pain. The baby kept descending. She squeezed her vagina tightly so she wouldn't push it through the canal until the doctor arrived.

"Wait, little one. I'm excited, but you've got to stay there a little longer." She patted her lower stomach. "Please, God, keep him or her in my womb a little longer."

Ten minutes later, Dr. Wright came in. He yawned, approached Tabbie, and shook her hand. "I'm Dr. Wright. I met your husband outside the door. I reassured him that I've delivered plenty of babies and that we'd do fine. Nurse, will you get Miss Tabbie a blanket, please? She's shivering."

"Of course," the nurse said. She reached into a cabinet and withdrew a nongender blanket, a yellow one.

"Let's take a look at our young mother here." He disappeared under a white sheet that the nurse had spread across Tabbie's legs. "It looks like the baby is beginning to descend. No time for an epidural. It's going to hurt a little." He patted Tabbie's hand. "But it won't last long. Scream if you need to."

The nurse held Tabbie's hand. Tabbie didn't know whether to keep her eyes open to see the doctor catch her baby or shut them to help with the pain. The nurse sensed the dilemma. "You can close your eyes, and I'll tell you when the baby is here."

"Push," Dr. Wright kept saying. "Push hard."

Tabbie pushed so hard she thought she might break a blood vessel. Then she heard a soft cry, and she started to cry. "Please get my husband."

"It's a little girl with red hair. Let me clean her up, wrap her in a blanket, and we'll get you to a room," the nurse said, smiling.

"Is she healthy?" Tabbie asked.

Dr. Wright answered, "She has all her toes and fingers. Her reflexes seem fine. You've got a lovely redhead. You know what they say about redheads. They're tigresses."

"I know. I've got a twin sister with red hair. Don't tell my husband about the hair color. I better tell him. He doesn't get along with my sister."

Fifteen minutes later, the nurse wheeled Tabbie and baby Carole, who had a pink cap on, into the hallway to see Daddy Eric.

Eric leaned down to take her. He held her tenderly. "She looks like you, Tabbie. She's beautiful. Let's take her cap off and see if she has hair."

"Wait until we get to the room, Eric. It's too cool in the hallway."

He put the baby back in Tabbie's arms, and the nurse wheeled them to room 21.

Once she got Tabbie comfortable in bed, she took the baby so she could weigh and measure her in the nursery. "I'll bring her back in ten minutes."

"Wait, I want to see her hair," Eric said, following the nurse into the hallway.

He returned to the room, looking pale. "She's got red hair. Damn! I don't want a replica of Dorcas." He looked helpless.

"Eric, hush," Tabbie said, reaching toward him. "She will be wonderful. We'll love her, encourage her kindness, and we'll set rules for her when she reaches the terrible twos. Dorcas was in charge at home, but I think Kate enjoyed her feistiness and encouraged it. We'll raise our baby differently. We'll teach her how to get along with others."

"If we call her Tabbie, then we know she'll be sweet." Eric sat on the edge of the bed, holding the baby, kissing her soft pink cheeks.

"I'm not sweet, Eric, I'm kind," Tabbie said, pinching his arm. "And remember that we decided to call her Carole, after my grandmother. I wish you had known her. She played tag, bought us coloring books, and even got on all fours looking under the bed when we played hide-and-go-seek. Phoebe is like her."

"Why don't we name the baby Phoebe?" he asked.

Tabbie started crying. She was exhausted from giving birth and tired of arguing with Eric. Eric put the baby back in her arms.

Dr. Wright and the nurse came in holding the birth certificate. "We need the name of this pretty little redhead," Dr. Wright said.

Eric said, "She's a pretty girl like her mom. Hair color has nothing to do with her." He wondered how old their daughter needed to be before Tabbie could change the color to brown.

"Her name is Carole Phoebe Stutsman," Tabbie said, yawning.

"I bet those are two special people in your family," the nurse said.

Tabbie nodded.

XXXXX

In June, Tabbie began to suspect that Baby Carole was deaf. She expected her beautiful curly redheaded Carole to follow all of Dr. Spock's guidelines of when to do what. Baby Carole might be ahead of them, she thought proudly. She was already playing paddy cake and sleeping through the night. But she wasn't imitating words, like *mama*, *baba*, which four-month-old babies should do.

Tabbie didn't tell Eric her suspicions. He was studying for the finals so he could graduate in his specialty, school administration. She began to write her fear and prayers in her journal at night. *God, please open Baby Carole's ears so she may hear our voices, birdsongs, and nursery rhymes. Lord, what did I do in my pregnancy that could have caused it?* She scanned her activities, which all seemed safe. *I think I'm wrong. She looks like one of the deaf twins I taught, and I'm getting them mixed up. Lord, please be with Carole, let her learn and let me love and teach her. Love, Tabbie.*

During the day, Tabbie played games with Carole that tested her hearing. When Carole was in the crib, sitting and holding on to the wooden slats, Tabbie would pop up from the floor and say, "Boo." Carole would laugh, clap her hands, and fall on the mattress.

"Mama Boo," Tabbie repeated. "Carole, say, 'Mama Boo.'" She encouraged her sweet baby. Carole didn't make a sound.

When it was time to eat, Tabbie picked her up and put her in the infant seat on the table. She pulled her own chair up and made noises. "Mama, baba, dada," she said. Carole didn't copy. Tabbie pressed Carole's warm little hand against her own lips and repeated, "Mama, mama." Carole laughed and shook her shoulders but didn't make a sound.

"Say something," Tabbie pleaded. "Then I'll know whether you hear me or not." Tabbie felt her heart thud down through her stomach to her feet. "It can't be. You're supposed to be perfect, cute, and healthy. I didn't pray for this." Tabbie laid her head on the table and cried. Carole patted her head. There were no comforting sounds, only silence.

Tabbie breathed in deeply and raised her head. She looked into Carole's happy face and kissed her. Then she opened the icebox to get strained carrots. She held them out to Carole. "Yum, yum," she said, heating them up. She told herself, "It's important for me to speak. I can't become mute also."

CHAPTER 11

On June 10, Eric walked onto the platform at his outdoor graduation to get his MS in Education Administration.

Tabbie, Phoebe, Richard, and Cindy sat in the bleachers in the sun. Cindy held Baby Carole, who wore a pink bonnet and a light sweater to keep her skin from burning. Tabbie helped her clap her hands as her daddy received his diploma from the dean of education. As Carole clapped, she grinned at the people behind her.

"What a quiet, sweet baby," a woman leaned over and whispered.

"Thank you," Tabbie said. Carole grasped Tabbie's breast and made a sucking sound. "She's hungry. Do you think it's all right for me to nurse her here?" Tabbie whispered to Phoebe.

"Of course. Cover yourself with her pink blanket, and let her go at it," Phoebe said. "I'm glad you're still nursing. She'll get fewer germs this way."

"It's too late. The damage is done," Tabbie said, wiping tears from her eyes.

"What do you mean, Tabbie?" Phoebe asked.

"At lunch, I'm going to tell Eric, you, Dad, and Cindy what I mean," she said, looking up as the last student marched across the platform.

Within five minutes, Eric had taken off his hot black robe and was looking for Tabbie in the bleachers.

"We're over here, Eric," Tabbie called out, waving.

Eric hurried over, handed his robe to Tabbie, and took Carole. "Are you proud of your daddy?' he asked, kissing her. She squirmed, smiled, and patted his cheek.

"Do you love your granddaddy?" Richard asked, lifting her into his arms. Carole smiled and yanked his hair.

"Ouch," he said, pulling her red hair lightly.

She leaned forward and twisted his nose. She fussed to go back to her daddy.

Eric took off her bonnet. "Do you like our redhead who's got a gentle spirit like Tabbie?" he asked, moving Carole around the family circle.

"Beautiful," Phoebe said.

"A little Tabbie with red hair. I don't see any of Dorcas in her," Richard said.

"When she's cross, she looks a little like my aunt Marion, my father's sister, but she was fussy and deaf," Eric said.

"You never told me about her?" Tabbie asked in disbelief. "Why haven't I met her?"

"She died when she was young. Too much meanness, my dad always said. My mother said that she got a spinal infection. It spread through her body and killed her."

Richard reached in a paper bag that was on the bench and pulled out a white carnation. He stuck it in Eric's navy blue pocket with its little white head poking out. Next, he brought out a small wrist corsage made of sweetheart pink roses and slipped it on Carole's wrist. "Pretty," he said. He leaned up close to her face and said, "Say pretty, little Carole."

She patted his face.

Cindy reached for Carole and tickled her. Carole gave a staccato laugh, ran out of breath, and started crying.

Richard took her back. "I'm proud to be a grandpa," he said. "I've made reservations for us to eat at the inn. I even told them that we need a highchair." He seemed pleased with himself. He enjoyed being a grandpa and knew that Dorcas would never give him grandchildren.

As they entered the inn, Eric waved to several students and their families. The waitress put them at a round table in the middle of the room.

"Can we have a quieter one in the corner, please?" Tabbie requested. "We've got some important things to discuss."

"Save the serious talk for later," the waitress suggested. "You don't want to spoil this young man's graduation day. Today's supposed to be all about him. In fact, we are giving out free desserts to the graduates. No serious talk, just toasts and congratulations." She led them to a table in the corner. "Here are the menus," she said, handing them to everyone. Your drink orders, please." She jotted them down as the family got comfortable in their seats.

Tabbie looked at everyone, cleared her throat, and started mid-sentence. "Baby Carole is deaf." She wiped her tears with her linen napkin.

"What? That's impossible," Eric said, leaning over to Carole and wrinkling his face.

Carole squealed and tried to wrinkle hers.

"There's nothing wrong with her. She's quiet, not a blabbermouth like your twin sister. I bet you were slow to talk, Tabbie, because of Dorcas pushing you aside to make her noises. Isn't that right, Richard?" he asked.

"You're right. Dorcas *baa*-ed loudly. We couldn't hear Tabbie's soft voice beneath Dorcas's trumpet sounds."

"Quiet. Will you let me speak?" Tabbie said loudly. "Carole is four months old and isn't imitating any sounds we say to her. Remember, I taught deaf children, and I know the signs to look for." She turned to Eric, took his hand, and said, "We have a deaf child, like your aunt Marion." She was frightened. She didn't know how Eric would respond. He worked so hard to get things right in his studies and in his love tasks for her around the house. He got frustrated when he couldn't fix something.

He shook his head. "You're wrong. What do you think, Aunt Phoebe?"

"I think it would be good to take her to an audiologist. He can do the test and let you know if she has inherited it. I think hereditary deafness is called autosomal deafness. A recessive gene passes it down."

Eric put his face close to Carole's again. "I'm your daddy. I love you. Say dada."

Baby Carole slapped her hand on his face and twisted his nose and cheeks. She laughed, but she didn't say the word.

His face turned to worry, and a few tears dropped. "You may be right, Tabbie. How could I do that to you?" He looked at her sympathetically. "When did you discover this? You're not supposed to keep secrets from me. You're supposed to share all your worries and fears." He scolded her, but he was mad at himself for fathering a deaf child. He breathed in deeply and apologized. "I'm sorry I came across mad. I love Carole and will do whatever you want me to do with her. I can learn to sign."

"Did you suspect it, Dad?" Tabbie asked her father. "You've babysat for her several times. Did you notice she wasn't babbling?"

"No. I'd feed her, she'd yawn, and I'd put her to sleep. I just thought she was an easy baby to care for. You and Dorcas were much more trouble," Richard said.

"Phoebe, you've been up every couple of weeks to see her. Did you suspect anything?"

"Yes," she said with hesitation. "It seemed to me she should have been imitating more sounds, but I didn't know what was wrong. I was waiting for you to tell me."

"What about you, Cindy?" Tabbie inquired.

"I've never taught a deaf child," Cindy responded. "I thought she was extremely quiet, an observer. Her eyes are so alert, noticing the smallest creature. She saw an ant on the table yesterday when she was eating her strained squash and pointed at it. I've nicknamed her Sharp Eyes."

Eric clapped his hands. "I have something to share with all of you. I interviewed for the job of assistant principal at Bradberry High School, and I got the job."

Tabbie screamed. "Now we can move back to Bradberry. We'll be close to Phoebe, and she can love on Carole the way grandmas do. Dad and Cindy can spoil her. Where shall we live, Eric?" she asked.

"Slow down, honey." He walked over, stood behind her, and pretended to pull on reins.

Eric sat opposite Tabbie. "In your journal, have you written to God to heal Carole? You tell me that help is possible when you pray to Him. I will pray too, but He may not recognize my voice. I don't talk to him often."

"God may not heal Carole's hearing, Eric, but we can pray that we raise her with love," she whispered, and hugged him.

"Yes," he said. "She doesn't have to be fussy and mean like my aunt who was deaf." He tickled Carole's tummy, and she laughed. "Tabbie, while I was over in Bradberry, I looked for houses in town. The only one for sale was the Thompsons' old home next to the library, and it's falling apart. I didn't have a chance to check out the small farmhouses on the back roads. We can do that together."

"Eric, when do you start working?" she asked, hoping it would be right away.

"He wants me to start in mid-July. That's two weeks from now. I'll spend Monday through Friday in Bradberry and come back to you and Carole on Friday nights."

Tabbie grimaced and shook her head. "You're not leaving us here. Don't forget, I grew up in Bradberry. If anyone goes there for the week, it's Carole and me."

"Slow down, Tabbie. Don't get so mad. We're discussing ideas. We haven't decided yet." He looked over to Richard or Phoebe for help. Neither of them said anything.

Tabbie lifted Carole from her high chair and put her in Phoebe's lap. "Aunt Phoebe, could we stay with you for a little while?"

"Of course you can. The longer the better."

Tabbie looked over at Phoebe, her dad, and Cindy with tears in her eyes. "I can't believe I have such a giving family. I thank all of you," she said, going around the table to hug everyone.

"Phoebe, I'll clean and cook for you until you get home from work," Tabbie said.

The waitress came, cleared the table, and brought Eric his apple pie à la mode. He sat Carole on his lap and gave her the first bite; she smiled at him, clapped, and leaned forward for another taste.

XXXXX

Tabbie, Eric and Carole moved into Phoebe's home the second weekend in July. Tabbie parked her station wagon in Phoebe's drive, and Eric drove a U-Haul behind it. Phoebe, who had been watching through the window, hurried out. She was wearing sneakers and her grandmother smock that had a cluster of plastic rainbow-colored keys, a little fuzzy duck, and a teddy bear, all safety-pinned on. "Give me Carole while you take the boxes and furniture to store at Mrs. White's," Phoebe said.

"Are you sure, Aunt Phoebe? She's wet and hungry."

"Hand me a diaper and a bottle. We'll be fine," Phoebe said, taking both and putting them in her smock's large pockets. She held her arms out and took Carole.

They heard the grind of gravel and saw Richard and Cindy's pickup pull in. "We're here to help you unload the heavy stuff," Richard said.

"Tabbie, you go in and lie down," Eric said. "I've got plenty of help."

Phoebe led Tabbie to Tabbie's old room; she had set up a crib near the bed. "Why don't both of you nap while I work on supper?"

Tabbie waved good-bye, put Carole in the crib, and lay down. They both fell asleep in five minutes.

In half an hour, Carole awoke, looked over at her mother, put her lips together, and moved them to say "Mama" but without a sound. She signed *Mommy* and went back to sleep.

Tabbie smiled in her sleep. She dreamed that Carole had said, "Mama."

CHAPTER 12

Tabbie and Eric stayed with Phoebe until the end of August. After searching for a small house to move into, they found a farmhouse a mile from Phoebe's. The older woman, whose farmer-husband had died five years earlier, had also passed away, and her children wanted to rent it. The lady had furnished the small rooms with sturdy New England furniture: an oak table in the dining room, a square pine table and chairs in the kitchen, and a formal uncomfortable floral couch and maple end tables in the living room. The house's exterior barn-red paint was beginning to peel, and Eric promised to paint it for a decrease in rent.

Tabbie and Eric moved Baby Carole's crib and toys into the downstairs bedroom and put a comfortable sofa and rocking chair in the living room for themselves.

The house had two downstairs bedrooms and a larger one upstairs. Eric decided to make the upstairs one his office and guest room and moved his desk into it. Tabbie gave Carole one of the downstairs rooms to sleep in, and she and Eric shared the other. Many nights when Carole fell asleep, Eric and she would go upstairs to make love in the double bed and return downstairs to the twin beds to sleep.

One night, Eric remarked playfully, "Tabbie, we could be as noisy as a freight train downstairs and Carole wouldn't hear."

"She can feel vibrations, Eric," she said, pushing him off the bed.
"Ouch, help me up, Tabbie. What's wrong with you?"
"I don't like you to make fun of our daughter."

XXXXX

In the last part of February, the wind whistled through the cracks in the windows of Tabbie's and Eric's house; heavy snow was falling. Tabbie sat at the table writing Carole's two-year-old birthday invitations, and Carole perched in her high chair scribbling on paper with wide crayons. Tabbie signed *party*, waving her hands in the air as if she were a music conductor. Carole looked through a Little Golden Book about a birthday party, turning pages with pictures of balloons, presents, cake, and ice cream. She banged on the table for her mother to put her on the floor and went into the kitchen to find a cake and wrapped gifts. She shook her head no and started to cry.

Tabbie picked her up and jostled her. Carole didn't understand time; she had to wait a week to turn two. Tabbie brought out building blocks, which they stacked and knocked down. Soon Carole was laughing.

Several days later, Tabbie received phone calls from Richard, Bess, Phoebe, and Dorcas saying they could come. Kate declined, saying she was too busy.

On the birthday morning, Richard and Cindy arrived first. He brought a flower box full of dirt into the house. Eric was reading Carole a book about a rabbit, and looked up. "What are you are you bringing into the house, Richard?"

"Carole's present. These go with it." He held up a small plastic shovel, hoe, rake, and a real geranium.

"It's early March, and the ground is frozen, Richard. Carole isn't playing outside yet," Eric said.

"That's why I brought this tarp," Richard said, holding up a brown plastic sheet. "I'll spread it out in her room, and it will catch any dirt that spills."

"You don't know much about child development, do you? Carole is at the stage where she puts everything in her mouth, and she'll carry dirt all over the house."

"Let's see what Tabbie says about it," Richard said, shouting her name.

She came out of the kitchen, Carole following. "Do you approve of my present for Carole?" He pointed at the flower box. Carole saw it and ran over. She sat down to smell the red geranium and smiled. She raked her hands through the dirt and poured some in her hair.

"Dad, look what she's done. Now I have to give her another bath! Please take it outside." Before removing it outdoors, Richard handed Carole a cardboard book of a little mole digging up plants and pulling them into his tunnel. Carole laughed and crawled under the chairs, pretending to be a mole.

"Can't get it right every time," Richard said, taking the box outdoors. "In the spring, she'll love digging in the dirt. We'll plant seeds, water them, and pick flowers for your vases, Tabbie. I've got a watering can in the car now. I'll get it."

"Wait, Dad. I don't want her pouring water all over the furniture. Keep it there until summer," Tabbie said.

They heard the outside door open, and Bess entered. "Where's my birthday girl?" she asked, looking around. She was carrying a small plush chair that Carole could sit in, and a stuffed cat.

"Tabbie is bathing, Carole," Cindy said. 'They'll be downstairs in a minute."

The outside door opened again, and Phoebe came in singing "Happy Birthday to you" and carrying two gifts.

A minute later, Tabbie appeared with Carole, who was dressed in a green corduroy dress, white blouse, and black patent leather shoes. Carole saw Phoebe and ran over to her to take her gifts. She unwrapped the bulky one and took out a wooden bird feeder. Sunflower seeds were scattered in the bottom. Carole began to chew on them and spit them out. *Bad.* She wrinkled her nose. *Me eat,* she signed, and ran to the table.

For lunch, Tabbie had made turkey sandwiches and cut-up apples.

As the family was eating, they heard a car horn. Phoebe stood up and looked out. "Dorcas has arrived carrying a miniature red car," she announced.

Dorcas came inside, dressed in bright red boots, a coat, and gloves. *I have something for my charming niece*, she signed.

Tabbie stared at her with a look of surprise and pleasure. "Dorcas, I didn't know you knew how to sign!" she exclaimed.

"I told you when I came to Carole's first birthday party and saw her red hair and how much she looked like me that I'd learn. I have an American Sign Language book and practice in the bathtub when I'm taking one of my forty-minute soaks. In fact, I'm working on my third book. The first two fell in the tub when I dozed." Dorcas put the red car beneath Carole's highchair. *A car for my Carole*, she signed.

Carole looked at it, lifted her arms up to Dorcas to get her down; she climbed over the sides and onto the seat. *Go*, she signed, and pushed it forward with her feet. Everyone clapped and signed, *Go*.

Carole drove the car through the living room, bumping into chairs. She signed *Bad chair* when she got stuck, and climbed out to kick it. Dorcas showed her how to go backward, but Carole signed no and tried to move the bulky chair. Her frustration grew, and she burst into tears. Dorcas picked her up, kissed her wet cheeks, and took her outside where they both climbed in the driver's seat of her car. They twisted the steering wheel, and Dorcas pressed on the horn. It blared, but only the family inside heard.

Eric went to the door and yelled, "Dorcas, bring the birthday girl in. The candles on her cake are already lit."

When they re-entered the house, Carole ran to her high chair where she saw a double-layered chocolate cake with two glowing candles on it. Tabbie signed *Happy birthday* while everyone else sang it in different keys.

Richard said, "Signing is more melodic."

Tabbie quickly blew out the candles as Carole reached for them. She grabbed a piece of cake with her hand and stuffed it in her mouth.

"Someone likes chocolate as much as I do," Richard said, going over to lick the hand that Carole wasn't licking.

"Save some for me," Eric said, coming over and licking Carole's cheeks.

"All right, chocoholics," Phoebe said, tapping each of their heads with a kitchen knife. I'll cut you your own piece."

CHAPTER 14

Tabbie and Eric greeted nine-pound roly-poly Ricky in April 1968. Carole, age three, was certain that he belonged to her; she threw her rubber doll in the wastebasket and demanded to rock and kiss his little lips. Tabbie rescued the doll, pulling her out of the trash, and signed, *two babies and two mommies*. When Carole saw Tabbie lift her blouse and nurse Baby Ricky, she lifted her floral shirt to nurse her baby, Rose.

When Ricky was a week old, Tabbie called Dorcas to tell her about his arrival.

"Is he deaf?" Dorcas asked.

"No," Tabbie answered. "His eyes, ears, and nose seem fine."

Dorcas coughed and said, "Then I can't love him as much as Carole."

"Dorcas, why do you like children with handicaps? You're so particular about the friends you choose. They have to be smart like you, or smarter."

"By liking injured children, I'm proving to myself and others that I'm not the snob that most people think I am."

Tabbie shook her head; even though she and Dorcas grew up together, Dorcas still confused her. "To see him is to love him. He has Play-Doh cheeks that hide his eyes and a tuft of brown hair."

"Tabbie, I don't have time to be a ravishing aunt to both. He'll win a town full of hearts."

Tabbie wanted Dorcas to know that she was alone in exiling Ricky. "Dad is thrilled and is already planning what types of gardens to plant with him. Kate sounded relieved that we have a healthy baby boy, but she has already dismissed him because she thinks he resembles Dad. She said, 'If he has an artistic personality and shows tendencies to be like Ronald, then I'll swoop down and carry him off.'"

"We're all different, aren't we, Tabbie, but I'm happy for you that he's normal. What does Carole think about Ricky? Is she jealous?" Dorcas asked.

"A little. She has decided to go back to diapers instead of using the potty chair. But I've read in Dr. Spock that's normal."

"I have to go, Tabbie. I'm late for a rehearsal. I hope that you've noticed that I'm sweeter to you. I'm full of surprises." Dorcas laughed and hung up.

For an instant, Tabbie felt nervous about Dorcas moving into her realm of kindness. She wasn't sure that she could ever travel into Dorcas's kingdom of brilliance. *But I am gaining everyday wisdom,* she told herself.

XXXXX

The first party that Ricky attended in his three-month-old life was Phoebe's retirement party in early July. At sixty-five, she had contributed fifteen years of excellent leadership as the principal of Bradberry Elementary School. She made curriculum changes, and now Bradberry students spent equal time in reading, grammar, and math instead of playground activities gulping up classroom time.

Cindy replaced Phoebe as principal. At forty-five, with her master's degree in education, the school board elected her unanimously. They said, "She can ask Miss Phoebe to help her solve school problems during supper or when they drink coffee in the morning."

"We're not losing Miss Phoebe," a board member pointed out. "We're gaining Miss Cindy."

After retirement, Phoebe spent afternoons with Tabbie, Carole, and Ricky. They walked across the road to let Carole feed sugar lumps and carrots to the farmers' horses behind the wire fence. When it rained, Phoebe and Carole put together wooden puzzles of horses, cows, and pigs while Ricky, in his swing, watched and babbled.

At the end of a hot, buggy July, the family who rented their house to Tabbie and Eric wanted to sell it. They offered it to Tabbie and Eric, but they declined. They wanted to find a house on East Hill Road, closer to Phoebe, but they got discouraged looking. They found only small trailers and one farm that was littered with falling-down chicken houses, abandoned cars, and a washing machine on the porch.

Tabbie called Aunt Phoebe. "We haven't seen anything on East Hill Road. We'll search in town and in Spitford, which is only ten miles away."

"Wait," Phoebe said. "Why don't you move into my house and I'll cohabit with Bess? God has given me the gift of health and energy, and I mean to use it helping you care for Ricky and Carole."

"It's not fair to you to have to put up with Bess, her cats, and her quirks."

"Whenever we get into a battle that lasts more than an hour, I'll come across the lawn to visit you. She'll be gone in the morning, working at the animal shelter in Glennsboro, and I'm helping out at the local public library in the afternoons," Phoebe said. "Absence makes the heart grow fonder, so it's a done deal."

Tabbie smiled. "Let me check with Eric tonight, and I'll give you an answer tomorrow." She hung up the phone and started to think up a strategy to win over Eric: food—rare steak with horseradish, cheese-baked potato, and asparagus drenched in Hollandaise sauce, twice a week; sleep—keep the house quiet until 10:30 a.m. on the weekends; a movie in Glennsboro twice a month; and a new 10-gear Schwinn for biking the country roads. "That will do it," she said, clapping her hands as she heard Carole banging on her crib and Ricky yelling, "Mama."

At 6:00 p.m., Tabbie was grilling a steak in the front yard while Carole was pushing Ricky in her red car. At six months, he could sit, but when she turned a sharp corner, it tipped, and Ricky fell out. Eric pulled into the drive, just in time to pick up his crying son and reach down to lift Carole into his other arm. Tabbie looked over; she loved Eric a pinch more when he held and kissed both Ricky and Carole. Sometimes Ricky got more tossing in the air and chasing on the floor.

That evening, while Tabbie cleaned the kitchen, she reviewed her morsels of enticement for Eric. She added one more: lovemaking twice a week. Eric finished reading an animal book to the children; he signed for Carole and made *oink-oink, neigh-neigh* sounds for Eric and put them to bed.

When he and Tabbie drank coffee on the porch, looking across the fields, she moved her wooden chair closer to him. "I want to propose—" she started.

"We're married, Tabbie. I proposed to you four years ago," he said, taking her hand and kissing it.

"It's a plan for where we can live, Eric. Aunt Phoebe is moving in with Aunt Bess, and she invited us to live in her house."

"Tabbie, think logically. Living with Bess would be like staying with Dorcas. Each is a bossy lunatic with crazy passions. I wouldn't subjugate Phoebe to sleeping with so many cats."

"Eric, wait. Listen to my plan."

After she outlined it, Eric laughed. "The part I like the most is lovemaking," he said, kissing her. Then he turned serious. "We've lived with her before, Tabbie. It's time to find our own place."

"We'll make it temporary, Eric, until we find our own house. Until then, Carole can feed the horses in the field across the road, and Ricky can pick blueberries off her bushes."

"Let me think about it, and if you prove your promises, like making love tonight, it's a done deal," he said.

XXXXX

They moved the last week of August. The first month of September bounced along with a few mishaps. Several times Carole ran across the road to feed the horses without Tabbie or Phoebe. Tabbie spanked her and signed, *No, Mommy go with Carole to see horse.*

Ricky grew into a happy, quiet baby. When he became a one-year-old and Carole three-and-a-half, they found that he liked to toddle over and plop down on the fragile house she made with red and blue blocks; he was like a tornado, making them fall apart. *Bad boy*, she signed, and spanked his padded bottom. He hugged her and threw a green block at her; Carole bit him if Tabbie were in another room.

In the mornings, Phoebe took Carole out to ride her tricycle. She liked to ride across the road to feed carrots to the horses, and Phoebe walked beside her.

XXXXX

One afternoon, when Carole and Ricky were napping, Tabbie wrote in her journal. *Dear Lord, I love playing games with Ricky. My heart melts when I hear him say "Baba" and "Mama" and when we play peekaboo. I'm having more fun with him than Carole. Forgive me, Lord.* She ended the page.

Later that night, when Phoebe put Carole to bed, Tabbie bathed Ricky, who splashed bubbles all over her and screamed with delight. Tabbie leaned over to rub his tummy with her head. "I love you, Ricky," she said. He beamed at her, pulling her hair and saying "Mama" as she dried him with a towel. She rocked him asleep and laid him in his crib.

In the kitchen, she poured herself a cup of coffee and joined Phoebe and Eric in the living room. She sat next to Eric and laid her head on his shoulders. "I'm a bad mom." She sighed. "I think I love Ricky more than Carole. When he says 'Mama' or claps his hands, I laugh and tickle him. Carole comes over and sits on him. I get so tired of correcting her."

Phoebe stayed quiet and let Eric answer her. "It's natural, honey, to fall in love with Ricky. When I'm at school, I hear him say 'Da, da' in my mind and feel his warm cheek against mine. It makes my day go better."

"But Carole is our child too. We need to love her," Tabbie said, and pinched her hand the way she used to when she didn't like herself. She looked over at Phoebe. "I don't know what's happening to me. I sometimes want to give Carole away. She seems like more trouble and work than I can handle. Isn't that mean and uncaring? I'm getting all tangled up in my emotions."

Phoebe went over and hugged her. "Of course not, Tabbie. You work so hard at being a good mother to both. You are as tired and limp as a dust rag. I think it's time for Carole to start the preschool program at the School for the Deaf in Glennsboro. She'd delight in playing games with children her age, and she'd learn more signs. I'll pay for it if you and Eric can't."

When Tabbie heard Phoebe's idea, she grinned, imagining Carole coloring and climbing up small slides on the playground with other boys and girls.

"What do you think, Eric?" she asked.

"Sounds great," he said, kissing Tabbie. "Under one condition that you don't volunteer to help out. You need some time for yourself and Ricky."

"Along that line," Phoebe said, "I want you both to flee for a weekend, and I'll watch them. I'll ask Grandpa Richard and Cindy to help."

"We can go to Boston and watch hockey," Eric said, whacking an imaginary puck with a stick.

"Or go to New York City and see a play that neither Dorcas nor Kate are in," Tabbie added. That began the pattern of one getaway weekend every two months.

In October, Carole started going to the School for the Deaf three mornings a week. She came home happy, signing in short sentences and wanting her new friend, naughty Nicky, to come to her house to play.

Tabbie was thrilled that Carole had found a friend she could sign and play with. She called Carole's teacher to inquire about Nicky's naughtiness and to ask for his mother's name and telephone number.

Helen, the teacher for the five-year-olds, reassured Tabbie he liked to play silly pranks on Carole, like hiding her hat in her boots. "They're like Tom and Jerry."

"What town does he live in?" Tabbie asked.

"Grafton, right between Bradberry and Glennsboro. His mother's name is Beth. She's a lovely woman whose patience and love for Nicky reaches the height of an airplane and the depth of a submarine. Her telephone number is 802-756-4113."

Tabbie called Beth that night.

Beth answered.

"Hello, Beth. This is Tabbie Stutsman, Carole's mother. She and Nicky have become close friends at the School for the Deaf. Carole wants him to come and play at our house in Bradberry. Can we plan an afternoon that works for both of us?"

"Tabbie, that sounds delightful; Nicky signs about her all the time. Why don't you and Carole come by tomorrow? I own and run a small gift store in Grafton. I work there from 10 a.m. to 3 p.m. daily. My mother picks up Nicky at 3 p.m., and when they return, she and my oldest daughter, Frances, run the shop while I 'harness' Nicky and prepare supper. He's an active one! We live in a small red house behind the shop. The front yard has a wooden fence."

"Thank you, Beth. We'd love to come. I'm surprised we haven't met at the school, picking up the kids."

"My mother, who lives with us, picks him up. She is a spunky, deaf, gray-haired woman. Ricky and she sign like dolphins."

"Oh, I know who she is. She seems to have more energy than Carole and Nicky pasted together."

"Yes. He inherited his nimble fingers and deafness from her. They both have magnetic personalities and mouths that move but don't make sense." Beth laughed.

"Do you want me to pick up Nicky tomorrow and bring him home?" Tabbie asked.

"No thanks. Consistency keeps him stable, and he expects his granny to drive him."

When Tabbie hung up, she wiped tears of thankfulness from her face. "Thank you, God. I've found a friend who can share the sorrow and challenge of rearing a deaf child."

She couldn't wait to tell Eric, Phoebe, Richard, and Cindy. As she planned her next phone call, she suddenly realized that she hadn't told Beth about Ricky. She called back. "Beth, it's Tabbie. I forgot to tell you that I have a three-year-old son named Ricky. Do you want me to bring him along? If not, I can ask my great aunt Phoebe to keep him."

"Bring them both. If she's a shopper, she can stop by the store. We sell crafts, candy, cards, and books by local authors. She can visit with my mother. Does she sign?"

"She's been learning the past five years."

"Great. Mom has been learning to speak a few words. They'll be a great match."

XXXXX

Tabbie called the family that night; everyone seemed pleased. She even called Dorcas. "Guess what, Dorcas? Carole has a new playmate at school named Nicky. They're playing at each other's house once a week. She's as passionate about him as you are about acting."

"Sounds wonderful, Tabbie. Why don't you start them acting? *Hansel and Gretel* would be a good one to begin with. Phoebe can help you with costumes, and Dad and Eric can make the sets. You and I, in abstentia, can be the directors."

"I'll think about it, Dorcas. Good night."

The next day, Phoebe declined the invitation; she wasn't feeling well. When Tabbie picked up Carole at school, she signed to Nicky's grandmother. *I am Carole's mother. We are going to visit you and your daughter today. I hope you like fudge brownies. I've got some in the car.*

I don't need them, she signed, *but I will devour them gladly.*

Me too, Nicky signed, and Carole added, *me too.*

Why don't you follow us home? Nicky's granny signed.

I go with Nicky, Carole signed, running after him to a red station wagon.

Carole and Nicky played tag, hopscotch, and climbed swing-set ladders with few falls. Tabbie and Beth shared stories of their children's deafness in spoken words.

"Where did Carole's come from?" Beth asked. "I knew I had a chance that one of my children might inherit it from my mother. My daughter, Frances, can hear, so I tried again for a hearing child, but it didn't happen. What about you?"

"Carole's deafness was a total surprise. Once she was born, my husband, Eric, told me he had an aunt who couldn't hear. She was so crotchety that he blocked her out of his memory, until Carole came.

"What was it like being reared by a deaf mother?" Tabbie asked. "Or maybe I should ask what it's like for Francis to grow up with a deaf brother."

"As an older sister, she loves and protects him, but she tells him to get lost when she's hanging out with her friends."

"Ricky would play with Carole all day if she would let him, but she runs into her room and locks the door when he messes with her puzzles or paint. He can pound on the door, or I can knock without action! We have an extra key."

After brownies and Kool-Aid, Tabbie walked Carole to the car. "Next week it's at our house," Tabbie said, as Carole and Nicky hugged good-bye. Nicky bit Carole's ear lightly, living up to his name, Naughty Nicky.

As Tabbie backed out the driveway, she stopped and drove forward. "I wanted to ask you about your fence. Does that keep Nicky from escaping your watch?"

"Yes, but he's working on climbing over it. We may add a little more height."

On the way home, Tabbie wondered about asking Eric to build one. "Our road is more country, less dangerous," she decided. When she got to Bradberry, she stopped by Smoky's. "Is my sign ready?" she asked.

"Finished it yesterday." He handed her a sign that said, "Slow—Deaf Child Playing."

"Can you change it to 'Deaf Children Playing?' Carole has a friend now."

"Sure," Smoky said. "Stop by in a week."

"How about Monday? He's coming over Tuesday."

"Consider it done."

Within a month, Carole and Nicky were like chipmunks going from one house to the other on Tuesday. Their trikes, puzzles, and balls went with them.

CHAPTER 14

The following fall, maple leaves splashed the air with red, yellow, and orange. Grandpa Richard brought Carole a small rake and toy lawn mower. Together they piled leaves and jumped in them. He brought three-year-old Ricky a toy with colored balls in a plastic globe that popped like popcorn when he pushed it. He laughed when he heard the noise and sat down to examine and pull it apart. The toy had no appeal for Carole who couldn't hear the pops.

By late October, Tabbie and Eric had gathered a gallon of McIntosh apples off the tree behind the house. Picking apples became a family game. Ricky treated them like small red balls, which he threw and kicked. When he lifted his leg, he lost his balance and fell. Carole sat down across from him, and they rolled round, red fruit back and forth to each other.

After ten minutes of this game, Carole bobbed down to pick one up in her teeth. She ran over to her mother and stuck it in her mouth. She threw one up to her dad, who was on a ladder in the tree, but a five-year-old's toss doesn't reach that high, and it came rolling back to her. She laughed, spanked the apple, and sat on top of it.

In early November, the frost and winds loosened the stems of the remaining apples, and they plopped on the ground. Carole took her pail outside and picked up the mushy apples. Phoebe and Tabbie watched her through the window while they folded clothes. As soon as Carole collected enough to fill her pail, she ran to the house and tapped on the windowpane, which was the signal for her mother to come and walk with her across the road to feed the horses.

Late one afternoon, Tabbie was dressing Ricky in his corduroy overalls when Carole tapped. Tabbie signed, *Wait, Mommy busy.*

The sun was setting, and the cold was coming in. Carole signed, *I feed horses.* She stomped across the lawn to the edge of the stony dirt road. Three horses galloped to the fence, neighing; Carole couldn't hear their pleading, but she saw their hoofs pawing the ground. *Three apples for three horses*, she signed and ran across the road. She didn't hear the old Chevrolet with oversized tires racing down the road; the driver, Sam Deaton, didn't see her. He and his twin brother, Dan, who had just revved up his old Dodge, were racing to the bottom of East Hill Road, each determined to win.

Carole couldn't hear the screech of tires or the radios blaring. Sam, racing into the lead, didn't see Carole; the car hit her. To Sam, it seemed like he ran into a bale of hay that fell off his father's truck. He sped on, honking, celebrating his lead position.

Tabbie thought she heard a car horn. "Let's help Sister feed the horseys," she told Ricky. "We'll put on your new jacket, the one Daddy gave you." Eric didn't want him to wear Carole's outgrown pink snowsuit, so he bought a navy blue one with matching scarf and mittens.

As Tabbie struggled to fit his arms in the sleeves, she looked out the window and didn't see Carole. She walked Ricky outside, saying, "Where's Sister? Find Sister."

Tabbie looked across the road to see if Carole was feeding the horses. She wasn't there. "She might have climbed through the gaps in the fence so she could gallop around," Tabbie said. She walked Ricky through the grass that the frost had pressed down. When they reached the road, Ricky ran.

"Sister fall," he said, bending over Carole, who was stretched out on her stomach. Blood marked her forehead and matted her red bangs.

"Carole!" Tabbie screamed. She tried to pull Ricky back, but he was already climbing on top of her, signing, *Sister play game.* When he saw blood on Carole, he leaned down and licked it, the way he did when he got a mosquito bite or scratched his leg. "Sister hurt?"

"Carole, my baby!" Tabbie shrieked, turning her over. Blood streamed from her nose; bruises discolored her face. Tabbie leaned over and did resuscitation, pressing on Carole's chest and breathing into her mouth. No movement. "Oh, Ricky, I think your sister is dead." She began kissing Carole's neck, arms, and hands.

Ricky pushed her aside and copied her.

"Play sister," he commanded, taking Carole's hand and trying to pull her up.

Tabbie sobbed. "She's asleep. Sister is sleeping in heaven with God."

Ricky started crying. "Sister, Sister."

Tabbie yelled. "I bet one of Farmer Deaton's sons ran over her. I heard the car honking. He is a murderer—a mean, horrible murderer!"

Ricky looked around for him. "Bad, mean boy!"

"Oh, Ricky, let's pray." Tabbie kneeled beside Carole; gravel cut into her knees. She put Ricky in her lap and folded his hands. "Oh, Lord. I hope you know how to sign. My little deaf girl, Carole, is coming to see you. She is sweet and energetic and loves to play. Maybe you can take her deafness away so she can talk and laugh with your other children. I can hear her shouting, 'Try to catch me,' and running like a horse."

Tabbie heard a truck coming down the road. Quickly she picked up Ricky, sat him at the side of the road, and gave him an apple. She hurried back to get Carole, lifted her limp child, and laid her beside Ricky.

Eric's gray pickup stopped. She ran over to his truck and knocked on the window.

"Oh, Eric," Tabbie sobbed. "Carole is dead. I think Farmer Deaton's son ran over her. She's dead, Eric. How could it happen? We should have built a wooden fence. It's our fault."

Eric jumped out of the truck and knelt over Carole. He lifted her left hand and felt her pulse—no movement. He opened her limp eyelids; her pupils didn't move. He lowered himself to listen to her heart—no sound. His skin paled. "Climb in the truck, Tabbie, and I'll lay her on your lap. We're going to the hospital." He lifted Ricky behind the steering wheel and started down East Hill Road.

"Wait, Eric." Tabbie yanked his arm. "Let's take her home. Once the emergency room team gets hold of her, she's no longer ours. She becomes theirs."

Eric breathed in deeply and repeated in a calm voice, "We are taking her to the hospital. The doctors may be able to resuscitate her."

Tabbie held Carole tightly as Eric drove down the steep hill; she didn't want her to roll onto the floor. "Do you think it's our fault?" she asked. "The sign wasn't enough. We should have built a fence."

"Don't blame yourself, Tabbie, you'll become depressed. Ricky and I need your strength and hope."

"And I'll need yours and God's," she said, stroking his arm.

Ricky looked over at her. "Mommy, don't touch Daddy. He have an accident."

When Eric reached the bottom of the hill, he skidded to a stop to avoid crashing into a logging truck passing in front of them.

"Damn," he said. "This truck will slow down to ten miles per hour around the curves. I can't pass him, or we'll get hit by an oncoming car."

"Damn," Ricky copied him.

"Don't say *damn*, Ricky. Say *shucks*," Tabbie said.

Twenty minutes later, Eric drove to the emergency room door.

An ambulance was backing up, and the driver honked loudly and shook his finger and head at Eric.

Eric gave him the finger and kept driving; when he reached the door, a medic met him with a stretcher.

Eric climbed out of his truck. "It's my daughter. A car ran over her! Please help."

"We'll take care of her. Sir, please move your car. This is reserved for ambulances."

"I'm not moving until you put her on your stretcher," Eric said. "She's on the seat."

"Move out of the way, sir," the medic said, pushing Eric aside.

Tabbie jumped out. "I'll go with you," she said, walking beside the stretcher, holding Carole's hand. She looked so small and alone.

"Me too," Ricky said, trying to climb up on the white sheets.

Eric grabbed him before he fell.

"Eric, will you take care of Ricky while I stay with Carole? The siren sounds, flashing lights, doctors and nurses shouting orders may scare him."

"They won't scare him. He'll be in the middle directing traffic," he said proudly.

"You two brave men do what you have to do. I'll call you if I need you," Tabbie said, following the nurse, medic, and Carole behind a green curtain.

Quickly the medical team checked Carole's heart, injected needles with clear fluid into her wrists, and wrapped Velcro bands around her arms to monitor her heartbeat; instead of sand-dune peaks and valleys, the sketch on the screen was flat.

An intern walked in, checked the notes the medic had scribbled, put his stethoscope to Carole's chest, lifted her wrist to get a pulse, and shook his head. "You can pull the blanket up and call the coroner," he told the nurse. He turned to Tabbie and said, "I'm afraid your daughter is dead."

Tabbie breathed in deeply and exhaled sobs and pleas. "Please get my husband and small son. They are probably at the bubble gum machine in the lobby."

Five minutes later, Eric came in with Ricky in his arms. Ricky leaned over the stretcher, lifted the blanket, and said, "Peekaboo, sister."

Tabbie took Ricky. "Sister sleeping." She reached over to Eric and laid her head on his shoulders. He kissed her. "I can't let her go, Eric. Can we bury her in the backyard, next to Woody?"

"No, honey. The law requires a proper burial. You have a family plot in the graveyard behind the church."

The orderly came in, stood behind the stretcher, and began pushing it out.

"Where are you taking her?" Tabbie demanded, blocking the way.

"We need this space for another patient. We have called Tripp's Funeral Home, and they are on their way."

"You can't take her. Tomorrow is Tuesday, and Naughty Nicky is coming over to play. They are going to feed the horses together."

"Please move, miss," the orderly said. "Yours is not the only emergency."

Tabbie slapped the orderly. Ricky kicked him.

"Calm down, Tabbie. I know it hurts, but Carole belongs to Mr. Tripp now."

"She does not. She belongs to God!" she yelled. "I want to take her home for an hour so I can bathe and dress her."

"You can't, Tabbie. Let's go home so you can call the family and your friend, Beth."

Tabbie screamed and pounded Eric's chest. "You never listen to me."

Ricky stomped on his daddy's foot. "Listen to Mommy," he said.

Tabbie turned to the nurse. She breathed in deeply, trying to glue her emotions to her chest. "I'd like you to put my daughter in my car."

"I'm sorry. It's against medical regulations to take a body away from the hospital. The medical examiner has to see her and pronounce her dead. Then Mr. Tripp will come," a nurse explained, taking Tabbie's arm and gently moving her.

Tabbie wouldn't budge.

"Do you have medicine that could calm her down?" Eric whispered to the nurse.

"I'll check with the doctor," she said, walking off. In a minute, she returned carrying a bottle of pills. "These will help. It's enough for five days."

"Thank you." Eric scooped up Ricky, took Tabbie's hand, and pushed open the exit door.

Ricky beat his shoulder. "Me get down. Take Sister to car."

"Carole is sleeping here tonight," Eric said.

"We have to tell him the truth," Tabbie said, standing straight. "Sister has gone to heaven to be with God."

"Me want to go there with her."

"We are going to Aunt Phoebe's," Eric said, carrying Ricky to the truck and putting him in Tabbie's lap.

When they got there, Ricky opened the door and slipped to the ground. He ran to the front door and rang the doorbell.

Phoebe opened it and lifted him. "How nice to see you." She nuzzled him. "Where's Sister?"

"In heaven with God," he said, running to the toy chest.

Phoebe rushed over to Tabbie and signed the same question. *Where's Carole?*

Tabbie burst into tears. "A car ran over her. She is dead."

Phoebe gasped and looked up at Eric. He nodded.

"It's my fault. Eric and I never built a fence," Tabbie said, wiping tears with her wrist. "She must have tapped on the window, and I didn't hear her. I was drying Ricky's hair off with a towel. He had just stuck his head in the toilet bowl."

"Why did he do that?" Phoebe asked. "Never mind answering. Sit down on the couch, and I'll get you some Kleenex." She went into the kitchen and brought a box back. She sat down beside Tabbie and rocked her. "It's no one's fault."

Tabbie suddenly sat up. "I want to go to Mr. Tripps' funeral home right now. I can't leave Carole there alone. He doesn't sign. I will sit and rock her in the refrigerated room. Phoebe, can I borrow your ski parka, mittens, and hat?"

"Tabbie, you need some sleep. Mr. Tripp and his assistant will care for her. Tomorrow when we see her, she'll look like her cute, rambunctious self," Phoebe said.

"Oh, Phoebe, I love you. I'll need you a lot these next few months…and years," she added.

The phone rang. Eric picked it up. "Yes, sir. You found him? Where? What's the next step? All right. I'll come by the jail tomorrow to sign the papers. Good night." He turned to Tabbie. "Sherriff Bates has Sam Deaton."

"I hope he keeps him in jail forever," she said, glancing down at her watch. It read 9:00 p.m. Not quite the witching hour, but it felt like it. She stood up. "I need to call Dad," she said, going into the kitchen, picking up the phone receiver, and dialing. When she heard his voice, she said, "Dad, Carole is dead. I think Sam Deaton ran over her. She's dead."

"Wait, Tabbie, tell me again. What happened?" There was disbelief and tenderness in his voice.

"One of Farmer Deaton's sons, Sam, was racing down the road with his twin brother and didn't see her. He ran over her."

"He'll end up in prison. Where is she now?"

"At Tripp's Funeral Home," Tabbie said quietly. *It's not a home,* she thought angrily. *It's a refrigerator with a casket.* But the word *casket* sounded worse.

"Cindy and I will be right over," Richard said.

"It's late, Dad. Why don't you come tomorrow?"

Tabbie called Beth next. She wasn't in.

She dialed Dorcas. "Sister, it's Tabbie. I have something sad to tell you. Sit down." Tabbie gave Dorcas time to find a chair. "Carole is dead. A car hit her, and she is dead."

Dorcas didn't say anything. Tabbie heard her cough and sniffle but no words. Finally she said, "Tabbie, that couldn't have happened, as careful as you are. You follow her like a hound dog. Who—"

"One of the Deaton twins. He was racing his brother in his car and hit her."

"Did he stop?"

"He drove on. The sheriff said he's denying it, and so is the other brother."

Tabbie heard crying. "Carole was my beloved, a gift from God, even though I don't believe in Him. Tell me when the funeral is. I'll be there."

CHAPTER 15

On Friday, November 12, the sun shone brightly—a day that Carole would have loved to have fed apples to "her" horses. Tabbie planned the funeral outdoors in the cemetery behind the Congregational Church. Carole's small closed coffin lay underneath a green tent in front of two rows of collapsible metal chairs. Two bouquets of black-eyed Susans, daisies, and milkweed decorated it, all gathered from the fields around Phoebe's house.

The service started at 2:00 p.m. Tabbie and Eric stood beside the wooden coffin. Tabbie laid her hand near Carole's head as she whispered to Eric and Pastor Tate, "I want the service to start promptly at two." Richard and Cindy, who were seated in the front row, held a twisty, fretful Ricky; he scrambled to get off their laps and run to Tabbie.

"Let him come," Tabbie said, squatting to catch him in her arms.

"Ricky, open box to see Sister," he said.

"No, Ricky. Sister sleeping." Tabbie put her finger next to her mouth, making a *shh* sound.

Dorcas arrived at 1:45 p.m., walked up to Tabbie, and handed her a bouquet of white and red roses. "Why don't you put these on the coffin? They're so much prettier than those." She lifted the field flowers and put hers in their place.

Tabbie stopped her. "Your bouquet is lovely, Dorcas. We'll put it next to the grave," she said, handing them to Eric and instructing him where to put them.

"All right." Dorcas sighed, looking out to see who was seated in the "audience." Her mother and Ronald took up two seats in the front row, Kate dabbing her eyes with Kleenex.

Dorcas turned to Tabbie. "Mother's dramatic today," she whispered with disdain.

Bess rushed in, carrying a bundle of pussy willows. "Tabbie," she called out. "Put these on top of the coffin. Carole loved pussy willows. She always made the sign for *cat* and rubbed them on her face."

"Thank you, Bess. Please put them beside the field flowers."

Pastor Tate stepped up to the coffin, whispered something to Tabbie and Eric, and they sat down. Tabbie passed Ricky over to Phoebe, who gave him a yellow lollipop to quiet him. She smiled and whispered to Tabbie, "Carole's flowers are lovely. I remember how she loved pulling petals off daisies, and how she blew milkweed fluff and tried to catch it."

"I think you are the only one who understands. I wanted to put dandelion fluff on it too, but Eric said no."

Pastor Tate hushed the small group and began the service.

"We gather here today to celebrate Carole Stutsman's life. Our church has been here over two hundred years, and we don't know how many deaf children lie in this cemetery. But we do know that little Carole had a wonderful family and happy life. She signed to me often, and I'm sorry now that I never learned to sign back. She taught us many valuable lessons. She had energy that comes from a cheerful heart. She loved others. In her young life, she followed the Commandments and the Beatitudes. We are losing a fine Christian little girl who would have made a fine Christian woman. Let us pray. 'God, please let our little Carole ascend to you and find a healed body in heaven. Let her hear your angels sing. Let her join their choir. Give her peace. Amen.' The parents have asked that we proceed with the burial without any remarks from this gathering. They welcome anyone to come up to their home for coffee and cookies afterwards."

"Ricky eat cookies?" He looked up at his mother, who was crying.

Several men lowered the coffin into the ground.

"You can come up now and put a handful of dirt over the coffin," Pastor Tate said, leaning over, picking up a handful, and throwing it in.

Dorcas and Kate came up together. As they were throwing their handfuls, a wind came up and blew dirt in their faces and on their black dresses.

Ricky ran up, filled his fists with dirt, and threw one at Dorcas and one at Kate. "Play with me," he said.

Dorcas grabbed him. "I'm your aunt Dorcas. We are friends. I bring special presents to my friends." She tried to kiss him before he got loose.

Kate caught him and spanked his bottom. "You must learn some manners, young man."

"Say you're sorry," Tabbie said, taking his hand.

"Sorry," he said.

"I'm sorry for his behavior. He's upset. He doesn't understand where Carole is. Come up to the house for coffee, and Eric will keep him busy."

"Thank you, Tabbie, but Ronald has to get back to Hepburn to direct a rehearsal tonight." Kate leaned over and kissed the top of her head. "I'm sorry about Carole."

"Thank you for coming, Kate," Tabbie said, giving her mother a light kiss on the cheek. She turned to Dorcas. "Come to the house and watch Ricky play with the toys you gave Carole. He loves the horse."

"I need to get back for tonight's play. If I leave now, I'll get to the theater in time to slip on my costume and paint my face. Please save me some pictures of Carole. I want to get them blown up and put them on my wall."

"Carole loved you, and so do we. Come back to see us." Tabbie opened her arms and hugged Dorcas. They both were crying as Dorcas waved good-bye.

Tabbie searched for peace during the winter. She tried to forgive Sam Deaton, who went off to the state penitentiary for vehicular homicide. She tried to wake up joyfully when she heard Ricky calling from his bedroom, "Mommy, you and me go feed horses." She tried to change Carole's room into a guest room and move out her bed, toys, and small table where she crayoned. She gave those to Nicky.

She and Beth brought their boys together every Wednesday. Ricky signed simple words, and Beth interpreted Nicky's signs when needed. Tabbie lived on Beth's support and love. Her cheeks had turned red with a crying rash. Ricky gave her a blankie to comfort her. Eric held her, wiped her wet cheeks with Kleenex, and listened to her heartache moments, but Beth knew how to make her laugh, along with listening to her deep sighs and angry blasts.

Tabbie went back to her psychiatrist, Dr. McFarland, in Glennsboro. In the ten-year hiatus, he had aged. More gray hair appeared, but he maintained his weight and his cool manner of dressing in gray pants and a V-necked sweater that covered a starched blue shirt. She noticed that the pictures on his bookshelves had changed. His children seemed older and were married with children.

He gestured to he' chair, and in his fatherly smile and voice, he said, "Tabbie, tell me about yourself. You look well."

"You do also, Dr. McFarland. I married a special man, named Eric, six years ago. He is assistant principal of Bradberry High School. We had a beautiful daughter named Carole, who was deaf. Our son, Ricky, is three years old. I've been volunteering at the School for the Deaf in Glennsboro, two mornings a week."

He smiled. "I'm happy for you, Tabbie. How can I help you today?"

"Carole was run over by a car in front of our house, a month ago." She cried softly. He offered her a Kleenex, but she had brought some from Eric's box. Ricky had insisted that she bring his blankie, so she held that.

"I'm so sorry, Tabbie," he said, his face clouding over with sadness. "Tell me more, please."

"I'm still grieving. I alternate between sadness and anger at the neighbor boy who did it. He's in jail now."

"Tabbie, sadness won't wrap your heart in black forever. Some small part of you will always miss her, but you can transform the rest of you to yellow, the color of sunlight, energy, and joy. You can use your experience to help other families with deaf children."

Together, they explored what that could be. She already taught preschoolers at the Vermont School two mornings a week.

He looked at his watch. "I'm sorry, our session is over, Tabbie. You can share your ideas of how to move forward, next week."

That afternoon, she decided to increase her teaching to four mornings a week and save Wednesday to visit with her friend Beth. She called the school to check that out with them, and they were delighted. She enrolled Ricky in the three-year-old group.

That night, she cooked Eric a love supper of grilled steak and potatoes, beets, and cherry pie. Eric put Ricky to bed while she cleaned the kitchen. Then they sat down in the living room with coffee.

"Eric," she began, "I made a plan to increase teaching deaf children to four days a week."

"What are you going to do with Ricky?" he asked, surprised.

"Take him with me. He can learn more signs."

"Tabbie," he said angrily, "I told you that I want him to play with hearing children. Mrs. Hayes has started a playgroup for three-year-olds in her home. She used to teach first graders in Phoebe's school and is qualified and capable."

Tabbie stood up to him, and it felt good. "Eric, I want Ricky to be bilingual. Carole and Dorcas would love that."

"Tabbie, be reasonable. Carole is dead, and Dorcas does not exist in my book."

"Eric, please give me this. Our town, our country, our world excludes people who are deaf. We can change that. Ricky can be an ambassador for them."

Eric looked worried. "Tabbie, we're in a gridlock. We're tangling up. Do you want me to come to your next session with Dr. McFarland? He can help us work out a compromise."

"No, Eric. I'd be in the minority. I'd ask Phoebe in to balance it out."

Tabbie let him take a couple of days to think about it. The night before she went to see Dr. McFarland, she said to Eric, "When two people love each other as much as we do, we can certainly find a way to negotiate. Let's pray about it," she said, kissing him and lowering her head. "Lord, thank you for joining us together as husband and wife. Thank you for increasing the strength of our bond as we've walked through dark days. Please let us continue to support each other. Amen."

On Friday morning, she returned to Dr. McFarland and shared her plan.

He looked surprised. "Have you told Eric?"

She nodded. "He doesn't like the idea," she said, smiling guiltily.

He was quiet and said slowly, "Tabbie, you and I have discussed the importance of you and Eric working on mutual goals."

"Dr. McFarland, you've encouraged me to examine what I want and pursue it. I'm doing that right now."

He smiled. "You are strong, Tabbie, but I'm asking you to wait. Don't change anything right now."

Their time ended with his repeating his sentence, "I'm asking you to wait. Don't change anything right now."

CHAPTER 16

Five months after Carole's November death, Tabbie woke one morning with a strange feeling after an even weirder dream. She wrote in her journal, "I dreamt that a jealous actress plugged Dorcas's ears with cotton so she couldn't hear. When Dorcas pulled the cotton out, she still couldn't hear her own voice. The evil actress laughed and danced away."

"Weird," Tabbie wrote. "Dr. McFarland taught me that I am every part of my dream. Am I going deaf? No, deafness is a major part of my life."

Ricky began to cry from his room. "Mommy up? Mommy up?" he sobbed, rattling the door. She had hooked it from the outside to keep him in.

How different to hear a voice, Tabbie thought, as she unlocked his door.

"Mommy," he ran to her. "Ricky eat snack."

She remembered when Carole pounded on the door; she threw books and toys at it but wouldn't say a word.

For the next two weeks, Dorcas didn't call. It surprised Tabbie because since Carole's death, she had called every week. Dorcas had grown a sprig of kindness for Tabbie.

Tabbie decided to call her at 4:00 p.m. one April. She let the phone ring eight times without getting an answer. She called again the next day and the next. Her dream resurfaced; fear ballooned inside of her. *Something's wrong.*

She called Kate. "Kate, is Dorcas all right? I've dialed her continuously, but she doesn't pick up the phone."

"I talked to her a week ago, and she complained about her sinuses and throat. She was going to notify me if she needed me to play her part in her play. Her understudy was sick also. She hasn't called, so I imagine she's okay," Kate said.

"Thanks. Let me know if you hear anything." Tabbie hung up. That night, she dreamed about an unhappy producer twisting and cutting the nerves that led to Dorcas's ears. When Tabbie woke, she told Eric she needed to go to New York City for the weekend. "Would you watch Ricky?"

"Why don't you call the theater? It will save you a trip. I don't like you driving in that crazy traffic," Eric said.

"No, I want to visit her, Eric."

"Then take Phoebe with you," he suggested.

"She's going to visit a friend in Poughkeepsie, New York. I'll be fine."

Driving to New York City, Tabbie wondered what had happened to Dorcas. She imagined crazy possibilities. *Had she been attacked by a robber and fallen so hard on the sidewalk that she was unconscious in the hospital? Had a car hit her? She never waited for the traffic light to turn green in order to cross the street. In Dorcas's mind, the cars should wait for her. Maybe she had neglected to wear her flaming red sweater, which she wore to stop cars.*

Tabbie turned on the radio to quiet her tangled mind. She heard Beethoven's funeral march and switched stations. When she approached the city, she drove toward Gramercy Park, where Dorcas was still living. Hearing sirens, she pulled over to the right side of the street as an ambulance and police car whizzed by. The shrill noise and speed unnerved her.

She drove slowly and arrived safely ten minutes later. She parked in the underground parking lot, rode the elevator to the second floor, and knocked on Dorcas's door. No one answered.

An older woman with stooped shoulders, gray hair wound in tight curls, and a multitude of wrinkles came down the hall. She was dressed in a handsome green suit with flecks of yellow pollen on it. "Dorcas isn't feeling well. She has locked her door. You're her sister, Tabbie, aren't you?"

Tabbie nodded; she had met the woman before.

"I have a key right here," the woman said, looking in her purse. "Let me open it for you."

Tabbie thanked her and reached for the key.

"Oh, no," the lady said, holding it back. "This is mine. We watch out for each other. She keeps a copy of my key also."

Inside the dark apartment, Tabbie called out to Dorcas. "It's Tabbie, your sister. Are you okay?" No one answered. With increasing alarm, Tabbie went into Dorcas's bedroom; she was asleep. Her cheeks were puffy as if balloons were under them, and she looked pale as a pillowcase. Tabbie felt her forehead. It felt as warm as a heating pad. Dorcas coughed.

Tabbie shook her gently to wake her. "It's Tabbie, Dorcas. I've come to help you. How long have you been sick?"

Dorcas opened her eyes which were watery and bleary. "No hear." Dorcas pointed to her swollen glands. "Hurt."

Tabbie hadn't seen Dorcas's apartment in six months. Their mother, Kate, often made surprise visits, inspecting its tidiness. Obviously, she hadn't come by lately because a pair of red heels lay on the glass table. A chair was turned upside down in the small kitchen; an empty coffee cup and a moldy slice of nut bread lay on the countertop.

Tabbie looked back at Dorcas's lumpy cheeks. "You've got mumps. Have you seen a doctor?"

Dorcas shook her head. "No hear. Write." She pushed a pad and pen toward Tabbie.

Tabbie wrote, "Dorcas, you have the mumps. Remember when I had them when we were eight? Dr. Otley wanted you to get the mumps also. He said complications can occur when you're older; men can become sterile and hearing can be affected in both genders. I coughed in your face and you used my spoons, but you still didn't get them."

Tears spilled from Dorcas' eyes. She picked up a red pen and wrote in large letters, "Mumps. No hear. No act. Sad and mad!" She coughed and shook her head. "No hear words. Deaf." She started to sob. "Deaf like Carole," she wrote.

Tabbie wrote, *Dorcas, I'll take you to a doctor. Do you have one in New York?*

Dorcas shook her head.

Where is your phone book? We'll find an audiologist, Tabbie signed.

Dorcas closed her eyes and shook her head. *I deaf. I mumps. Doctor can't fix me*, she signed.

Tabbie went over and opened her eyes. *We have to try*, she signed. Tabbie wrote another note and handed it to Dorcas. *I am going to take you home.* Tabbie opened Dorcas's closet and found a small suitcase. She opened drawers, removed two red cotton blouses, and took two pairs of red pants off hangars.

Dorcas watched from her bed. *I'm not going to wear red. It's a happy color for actresses*, she signed. *I no happy. I no actress.*

Tabbie exchanged the pants for gray ones and the blouses for black ones. She put them in the suitcase and shut the latches.

It was 2:00 p.m., and Tabbie was hungry. She found an apple and banana in the kitchen, which she ate, and returned to Dorcas to help her dress in a brown shirt and pants.

Dorcas shivered. *I cold. I need a coat*, she signed.

When they walked down the hall, Dorcas's neighbor came out her door and blocked the corridor. "Where are you taking her?" she asked in a protective voice.

"I'm taking her home. Home is where you want to be when you're sick," Tabbie said.

"Do you want to go?" the neighbor asked.

Dorcas shrugged, waved, and followed Tabbie.

In the garage, Tabbie helped Dorcas into the car. In thirty minutes, they were on the interstate. Cars whizzed by them. Tabbie drove a conservative fifty miles per hour. Drivers shook their fingers at her and honked. Dorcas dozed, gazed out her window, and dozed again.

Tabbie found it hard to sign and drive, and she couldn't write on her pad, so she settled into silence, which seemed strange because Dorcas usually filled every minute talking about her passion, acting.

Tabbie thought upsetting ideas. *Why would a caring God let this happen to Dorcas?* When Carole was born, she had asked, "Why, Lord, is she deaf?" She searched for answers and had never found them. She had changed her question to "Show me how to love her, Lord. And she had spent five years of her life helping Carole and her friends." Now, she prayed to find a way to love her sister who had tangled her up so many times. She slowed the car down, drove over to the right side of the road, and parked out of the way of speeding cars. She put her hand on Dorcas's lap and signed, *Don't give up, Dorcas. You can alter your dreams. Why not teach drama to the students at the School for the Deaf in Glennsboro?*

Dorcas shook her head and signed, *I will end my life if I can't act.*

You're stronger than that, Dorcas. Deaf children need a person like you to put drama into their lives.

I don't want to be a teacher. It's dull.

"You can teach dance," Tabbie said.

I can't hear notes, Dorcas signed, shaking her head in disgust.

How about writing? Tabbie signed with enthusiasm. *I wouldn't be alive if I didn't write my feelings and thoughts in a journal.*

That's your hobby, Dorcas signed.

God will tell you what to do. Listen to His voice.

I can't hear, and I don't believe in God. Dorcas fell asleep after that and woke up as they passed Bradberry's funeral home and courthouse on Main Street.

Tabbie drove slowly as Route 35 traffic merged into Route 30. *Where shall I take her?* she wondered. *Phoebe isn't home, and Bess doesn't sign. I don't want to take her to my house. Eric would explode, and she may still be contagious. I don't want Ricky to get mumps—or do I? It's better when he's young.* Tabbie drove up East Hill Road and pulled in her driveway. Eric and Ricky came out to greet them.

Ricky saw Dorcas, ran over to the car, and tapped on her window.

Eric pulled Tabbie aside after she got out of the car. "Why did you bring her here? She looks like death. She'll expose Ricky and me to whatever she has. I can't get sick now. Exams and graduation are coming up."

"Hush, Eric," Tabbie scolded. "Dorcas has mumps, which have left her deaf. You've already had them. I want Ricky to be exposed to them."

Eric gasped. "Not another deaf person in our family. We're spooked. You work with them all day. Ricky goes to preschool with them. We live in a hearing world, Tabbie. I wish you'd understand that."

"I'm going to put Dorcas in the guest room downstairs. If you can't be nice, I'll send you to Phoebe's."

Eric kissed Tabbie. "Sorry," he said, and helped Dorcas out of the car and into the house.

On Monday, Tabbie took a day off from work to drive Dorcas to Dr. Otley's office for a 1:00 p.m. appointment. Dorcas came out of her room dressed in her brown outfit. Tabbie lent her a bright green scarf, which Dorcas wrapped dramatically around her neck. She wrote on a pad of paper. *It's the Shakespeare swirl; our cast made it up. Has the producer of my play called? Has anyone called him? He must be furious at me for not showing up.*

Tabbie wrote back, *Kate told him. Your understudy is playing your part.*

To die or not to die, that is the question, Dorcas wrote.

Tabbie stopped breathing for a second and stared into Dorcas's brown eyes. *You're not going to take your life, sister!* she signed. Then she wrote, *Phoebe and I will help you find a new direction. You're creative and brilliant, sister. God has a plan for you. Going to see Dr. Otley is the first step.*

As Tabbie pulled up in front of Otley Hospital where Dr. Otley had moved his office, Tabbie prayed silently. *Let Dr. Otley and Dorcas get along. Keep their stubbornness at a minimum.* Tabbie parked, and Dorcas stepped out of the car and walked ahead of her.

She's still in the lead, Tabbie said to herself, smiling, as she followed her twin. *I can say whatever I want, and Dorcas can't hear.* She tried it. "Dorcas is a peacock, vain and selfish."

Dorcas didn't turn.

As Tabbie entered the building, she saw Dorcas was at the receptionist's desk writing a note.

Tabbie glanced at it. *My appointment is at one, and I will see Dr. Otley now,* Dorcas had written.

Nurse Starley had come into the waiting room, and Dorcas handed it to her.

She wrote on the pad in large letters. *He is at lunch. You will wait. Sit down.*

Tabbie took Dorcas's arm gently and signed, *Here is a chair we can use.*

Dorcas moved close to the entrance of Dr. Otley's office and stood. In ten minutes the door opened, and Dr. Otley appeared in his white coat and red bow tie. He walked over to Tabbie. "In your phone call, you said your sister had mumps and seems to be deaf?"

Dorcas stood up and turned in his direction. *Don't neglect me,* she signed.

Dr. Otley didn't understand; he had never learned to sign. She took a pad of paper out of her purse and wrote, *I'm the patient. I had mumps, and I can't hear. Examine me. Heal me.*

"Come in." He beckoned. "Tabbie, you come also. You can help me keep her tame."

Once they were in the examining room, he motioned for Dorcas to sit on the examining table. He looked in both ears. "They are red, infected, and swollen," he said to Tabbie. He handed Dorcas a heavy medical book. It was turned to a page headed "Hearing Loss after Mumps." Dorcas read it, looked up, and wrote on her pad. *Is there a remedy?*

He wrote back. *No, it's called SSNL. The prognosis is poor and recovery is unlikely.*

Dorcas stared at him, tears running down her cheeks.

He continued writing. *I'm not good at dealing with emotions. Your sister, Tabbie, and aunt Phoebe can help you with those. Dorcas, you're made of tough leather and will handle this fine. Good luck.* He put his pad in the drawer and turned to leave.

Dorcas wrote on his hand, *Thank you for giving me the truth, Dr. Otley.*

Let's go find Phoebe, Tabbie signed, and they left the office. *We will invite Dad and Cindy to supper tonight and tell them.*

What about Bess? Dorcas signed.

If you'd like, Tabbie signed back.

Dorcas nodded. *I want the whole tribe to know*, she wrote on a piece of paper.

That night, the family gathered at Tabbie's for supper. She made hamburgers, Phoebe brought cut tomatoes and lettuce, and Cindy and Richard brought french fries. Tabbie had put pads of paper and pencils at everyone's serving place.

"Are we playing Hangman?" Cindy asked. She and Richard enjoyed playing that game when they relaxed at home.

"No, Cindy. This is how we'll communicate with Dorcas. Dr. Otley said she is deaf with very little chance of recovery."

"Deaf!" Cindy exclaimed, glancing in Dorcas's direction. Dorcas was spreading mustard on her hamburger, oblivious to the talk around her. "How can that happen? With her constant talk, I would think she'd make other people deaf."

"Dr. Otley showed us an article in a medical book saying mumps could leave a person with an illness called SSNL, which is a hearing loss."

Richard looked at Dorcas in a hesitant way and wrote, *You aren't acting, are you?*

Dorcas wrote back, *Dad, this is permanent. I'm not acting. I'll never hear again.*

Cindy wrote, *Would an audiologist in Glennsboro or a surgeon in New York City, say anything more hopeful?*

"I'm going to take her to a specialist in New York City, next Monday," Tabbie said, looking at Eric to see his reaction.

"That's fine with me," he said, to Tabbie's surprise.

Bess said, "Tabbie, let me take Dorcas to her appointment. Even though I'm sixty, my friendship with Dorcas is stronger and less tangled than yours!"

"I can navigate the city better than you, Bess. I'm going to bring her back to Bradberry. New York City is too dangerous for a deaf person. Thieves can sneak up behind you and grab your purse. Dogs can growl and bite you. Bradberry is a friendly, slow-moving town," Tabbie said.

Unable to hear the conversation, Dorcas scanned each face for compassion. Phoebe's, her dad's, and Cindy's brimmed with empathy.

Bess moved and gave her a protective hug. "She's mine, and always has been."

Ricky got down from his chair, climbed into Dorcas's lap, pushed Bess's hand away, and said, "No, she's mine."

CHAPTER 17

Phoebe welcomed Dorcas into her home. She spoiled her by preparing meals, washing clothes, and dusting her room. Dorcas signed *Thank you* and wrote *Thank you* on her pad twenty times a day. She added a happy face on the paper, and her lips tipped up into a genuine smile when she signed.

Bess was ecstatic to have Dorcas living within shouting distance again. Of course, Dorcas couldn't hear her shouts, trumpet blasts, or car horn (her old ways to catch Dorcas's attention,) so she put on her sneakers and crossed the muddy lawn several times a day.

She wanted Dorcas to move in with her and her cat, Monkey Do, but Dorcas declined, signing, *Next door is close enough.* Bess's bossiness blossomed, and she took charge of planning Dorcas's weekends. On Friday evenings, she walked across the lawn carrying a chocolate cake and potato salad and ate with Phoebe and Dorcas. When they sat down, she pulled her pink pad of lined paper out of her jacket pocket. She had bought a rainbow of colors from the Bradberry pharmacy.

She tore off the top sheet and handed it to Dorcas. Bess spoke while Dorcas read it: "Saturday: One, wake at 8 o'clock. Two, eat breakfast in town at Maggie's Bakery. Three, drive to shelter and adopt Remus, a homeless orange tiger cat. Four, drive to Glennsboro to pick up canned and dry cat food and a catnip mouse. Five, eat lunch at Corner Sandwich Shoppe. Six, drive home to introduce Remus to Monkey Do."

Dorcas smiled at Bess and wrote, *Too much. Saturday I rest.*

Bess bristled. *I want you to teach me to sign so we can be friends again. When do you have time?*

At five o'clock, Monday, Wednesday, and Friday. We can teach our cats too. Practice bending your finger. It's necessary for signing.

During the week, Tabbie picked Dorcas up at 7:30 a.m. and drove Ricky and her to Glennsboro. Dorcas had started teaching acting to talented, eager deaf students, and they were working on a spring production of Helen Keller.

Dorcas hadn't visited Kate since her hearing loss. Kate had called Tabbie and complained about Dorcas's absence from the theater and her lack of phone calls. "Kate, she got a bad case of mumps and lost her hearing as a result. She moved back home and is living with Phoebe."

"Tell her to call me," Kate demanded, forgetting that Dorcas no longer talked on the phone. "Ask her to visit me in Hepburn. She's my daughter, and I need to see how serious her hearing has been affected."

"I'll give her your message. I've got to go cook supper, Kate. Good-bye."

"Wait, Tabbie, why don't you drive her over? You both can spend the night."

"That's not necessary, Kate. Dorcas drives her own car, the one you gave her."

"You've missed my point, Tabbie. I want to see you too. You're the daughter I hardly know. I'd like you to call me Mother again."

Tabbie swallowed in a startled way. "I'll call you tomorrow to let you know when we're coming."

On Monday night, as everyone ate together at Phoebe's house, Tabbie spoke and signed, "Kate wants Dorcas and me to drive to Hepburn to see her this weekend. She wants to see for herself that Dorcas is deaf."

"Seeing won't help at all," Eric said. He still hadn't learned to sign.

"Maybe she'll hit a spoon against the rim of a glass," Phoebe suggested, "or whisper a line from *Lady Macbeth*."

"Tabbie," Eric said, "you know I'm going to Montpelier to an education meeting. We had agreed that you would take care of Ricky."

"We'll keep him, Eric," Cindy and Richard offered. "It's time we go fishing in the pond. He'll love the wiggly worms on the hook and throwing the line into the water."

On Friday morning, Tabbie and Dorcas climbed into Dorcas's car with their overnight bags. Dorcas slipped in behind the steering wheel.

"Drive carefully," Phoebe signed, as she closed the door.

Dorcas drove slowly down East Hill Road onto Route 30 and reached her cruising speed of sixty miles per hour. Tabbie had brought her journal to write in, knowing that conversation would be impossible. An hour down the road, they both saw dark gray clouds bundling and billowing up in the skies.

Rain is coming, Tabbie signed.

Dorcas glanced over and nodded.

The first drops fell lightly.

Do you want me to drive? Tabbie signed and wrote on a pad, which she leaned against the steering wheel.

Dorcas shook her head no.

As the hill steepened, they drove into a low cloud full of fog and mist. Heavy rain poured down. Thunder drummed and sounded like gunfire in the distance. Lightning bolts flared like guns in a battle. Water flooded the road.

At the crest of the hill, a car moved slowly out of a driveway. The old woman driving stepped on her brakes, but her car slipped forward and hydroplaned. Her fear and confusion caused her to press on her gas pedal, just as Dorcas drove by.

Tabbie saw headlights come towards her; she felt a thump, a large bump that thrust her body forward against the dashboard; she heard a crash, the window glass shattered, she saw an image of Carole in front of her, and darkness descended.

Dorcas hurried out of the car and ran to her twin; in order to get to her, she had to squeeze between the lady's crushed bumper and the damaged passenger door; she climbed in beside Tabbie, whose head tilted limply to the right; her body, a floppy bag, leaned to the left. Dorcas picked up her wrist and felt her pulse. Nothing! She leaned over Tabbie's chest and pressed on it lightly as she put her lips to her mouth and breathed in and out. No breath!

She laid her head on Tabbie's chest, the way Tabbie used to put her head on hers when they were falling asleep as children. Dorcas used to push her sister off, saying, "Grow up. Move. I don't want your dandruff on me."

Now she signed, *I'm sorry, sister*, and held Tabbie softly. Two sisters finally untangled.

I want to thank the following people for their love and support, my husband, Travis Barnes, for listening and listening and listening, my 91-year-old friend, Sarah Lanier, encourager and critic, Molly McKitterick -editor of first draft, Sharon Smart, friend and english teacher, Table of Eight, for their encouragement, to Arian Jones, Publication Coordinator who kept the printing process moving and to God, who made all the difference.

ABOUT THE AUTHOR

Kathy Barnes, PhD, has a doctorate in marriage and family therapy. She has been counseling for twenty-two years and assists couples and families to untangle painful relationships. Kathy has a twin sister; they argue over who was born first. Unfortunately, their mother has dementia and doesn't remember.

Kathy has published three children's books: *Daddy Misses Kisses, Candy at War; Son, A Soldier's Work Is Never Done*. Her son is a lieutenant colonel in the Jag Corps and has served in Iraq and Afghanistan. Her other children's book is *Angels Protect Giraffes*.

Kathy worked as a preschool special education teacher and wrote, *Love Me, and Teach Me, Hug Me* for handicapped teens and their parents.

She has also published poems in several literary magazines.